Alexandra Michaels

Head of Catering
The Biltmore Hotel, Los Angeles

Elegant, unique and unforgettable weddings are my specialty.

Call for your personal consultation.

Please address questions and book requests to: Harlequin Reader Service
U.S.: 3010 Walden Ave., P.O. Box 1325, Buffalo, NY 14269
Canadian: P.O. Box 609, Fort Erie, Ont. L2A 5X3

Marriage, Inc.

ELDA MINGER
WEDDING OF THE YEAR

Harlequin Books

TORONTO • NEW YORK • LONDON
AMSTERDAM • PARIS • SYDNEY • HAMBURG
STOCKHOLM • ATHENS • TOKYO • MILAN
MADRID • WARSAW • BUDAPEST • AUCKLAND

HARLEQUIN BOOKS
225 Duncan Mill Road, Don Mills,
Ontario, Canada M3B 3K9

ISBN 0-373-30120-0

WEDDING OF THE YEAR

Copyright © 1989 by Elda Minger

Celebrity Wedding Certificates published by permission of
Donald Ray Pounders from *Celebrity Wedding Ceremonies.*

Printed in U.S.A.

A Letter from the Author

Dear Reader,

Weddings! Is there any one word that brings forth so many poignant images? Flowers, candlelight, the bride's beautiful dress. The perfect ceremony symbolizing the lifelong love and commitment between a man and a woman.

A very dear friend provided the inspiration for this novel. Sara is head of catering at the Biltmore Hotel in Los Angeles, and she has pulled off some spectacular celebrity weddings and formal dinners—including one dinner for the Duke and Duchess of York! I loved to hear stories about her job, and one night, over coffee, my heroine Alexandra was born.

I hope you have as much fun reading this story as I had writing it. Enjoy!

Elda Minger

Chapter One

The wedding of the year.

Alexandra Michaels stared out the window of her office, her gaze not focused on anything in particular. The Los Angeles sky was overcast, filled with dark gray clouds, and a steady rain had been coming down for the past hour. Yet nothing could dampen her elation.

Her intercom buzzed, and she walked over and pressed one of the buttons.

"Alex? Your mother's on the line."

Almost nothing.

"I'll take it." There was a quiet note of resignation in Alex's voice. She knew what conversation this was going to be. There were hundreds of variations on this particular theme. One thing about her mother, she was persistent.

"Alex? Darling, are you there?"

"I'm here." She was nervous already, hating the way her mother sometimes brought out the worst in her. The short, clipped voice. The defensive attitude. Why couldn't they treat each other as friends?

"Alex, your father and I just got back from London, and I wanted to let you know. How are you, darling?"

But Alex knew what that question really meant. Every

time she and her mother talked, a subtext ran in Alex's head.

This time was no exception.

"Darling? How are you?"

Is there an eligible man in your life?

"Fine, Mother. Just fine."

I'm not admitting to anything. Basically because I have nothing to admit.

"Oh. Well, what have you been up to?"

Please, Alex. Admit to having something of a social life. Lie to me.

Alex sighed and rubbed a finger against the side of her nose.

"Work, work and more work. But I do have some good news."

Mother, for once pay attention to something that's important to me.

"And what is that?"

Not the career again, Alex. You're thirty-seven years old, and according to the article I just read you have as much chance of getting married as of getting attacked by terrorists—

"I've got the Bradford wedding. They took my bid. I have three months to pull it all together, but this is definitely the wedding of the year."

"Alex, that's marvelous!"

Oh, I get it. There might be a nice, eligible, rich young man at the wedding ceremony—

"Darling, I— That *is* something to be proud of."

I'm trying, Alex, really I am.

"Thanks, Mother."

Ah, what the heck. Give her some hope. No sense in ruining her day because you've just about given up.

"Mother? You remember Karin, don't you?"

I do have a social life. I do I do I do.

"The girl who lives in the other half of the house? Of course, I do. Everyone always asks about the painting I bought from her. I hung it in the dining room."

"I went to a party she gave the other night—"

Oh, Alex! Maybe grandchildren...

"—I met some, I met this—"

Now don't get carried away—

"I met some people."

Brilliant.

"Anyone...special?"

A man?

"Ah...no."

In this town they're considered an endangered species.

"Well, don't give up." A comforting note crept into her mother's voice. "I was twenty-seven when I met your father, and people were convinced I was well on my way to being an old maid."

But I'm well on my way to being terminally single.

"I know, Mother. How was London?"

Can we get off this subject? Please?

Her mother chatted about her trip, Alex made soothing responses. Both agreed to call later in the week.

Then Alexandra Michaels, director of catering at the Los Angeles Biltmore Hotel, career woman *extraordinaire,* thirty-seven years old and celibate for the last fourteen months, hung up the phone and walked quietly into her private powder room.

Where she locked the door.

And burst into tears.

ONCE SHE ARRIVED HOME, Alex got her evening off to a grand start by talking to the cat.

"So I never meet a man, spend the rest of my life catering other people's good times and live here with you, Roscoe. Is that so bad a life?"

Roscoe, a hefty tabby tom, barely looked up from the can of salmon Fancy Feast he was devouring.

"Just like my ex-husband. He only came home to eat and clean up before he was out chasing anything but me."

Alex didn't have to look up to know her housemate, Karin, was standing in the doorway. They had bought the stucco duplex together and got along famously.

But at least Karin had something that passed for a social life.

"You," said Karin, plopping down on one of the breakfast nook chairs, "look like you've been talking to your mother."

Alex scanned her refrigerator as her friend spoke. She ate most of her meals at the hotel and barely had time to go grocery shopping to begin with. The fridge was depressingly empty.

"The scary part is that I'm beginning to agree with her. How many parties can I cater? How many weddings can I watch? I've been running as long as I can remember to get to where I am, and now that I'm there—"

"You need to get your valves blown out." Karin was grinning wickedly, swinging one of her long, tanned legs.

"Karin—"

"Your eggs fried—"

"I don't know about this—"

"You need to find a man who charges your battery, stokes your fire—I'm talking about *passion* with a capital *P.*"

"Who has time?" Alex was busily inspecting something wrapped in foil. It looked inedible, but at this point she was desperate.

"I made paella today. Jesse left for rehearsal already. Do you want to come over and have a decent meal?"

Alex pitched the piece of mystery meat into the trash. "I knew there was a reason I thought of you when I saw this house."

Karin stood up and stretched, then eyed Roscoe. "Just don't bring Muhammad Ali with you."

Roscoe had come with the house. Alex and Karin had found him the second day they moved in, parked on the back porch. Roscoe hated all other cats, period. Karin had two of her own, and Roscoe had taken them both on at different times, snarling, spitting and making sure fur flew.

He was not the most popular pet on the block.

But Alex didn't have the heart to get rid of him, and so each night she let him in the back door and fed him, and each night he followed her up the stairs and slept on the foot of her bed.

"He's inside for the night."

Karin's side of the house was huge. She had knocked out walls and painted everything white. Jesse, the main man in her life, had built her a platform in the living room so that the light for her painting was just right.

A multitalented woman, Karin also excelled at cooking. She had a vast collection of cookbooks, and this wasn't the first night she had taken pity on Alex and her empty refrigerator.

They were comic opposites, Alex petite and all curves while Karin was long-limbed and blond, with a perpetual tan. Karin played tennis and swam. Alex hyperventilated at aerobics. Karin ate mostly natural foods. Alex lived on coffee until Pierre, a chef at the Biltmore and a good friend, invariably brought up his newest creation around lunchtime. Karin lived in casual clothes or strolled around her house in her underwear. Alex lived in designer suits and classic shoes, her long dark hair carefully restrained in an array of flattering styles.

Karin was daring, Karin had Jesse, of the taut-muscled stomach and incredible shoulders. Of the dark, thick hair, smoldering Latin-lover eyes and full, sensual mouth.

Alex was not that daring. Alex had Roscoe, and though he had blazing yellow-green eyes and thick, tabby hair, he had a disturbing tendency to bring home fleas.

After dinner, the two women went back to Alex's side of the house and sat in the living room, glasses of wine in hand.

"So you've made it to the top, Alex. And so you're reassessing your goals. There's nothing unusual about that. I do it all the time with my painting."

"I guess I just feel like I've missed out on so much of life. It's like a horse wearing blinders, you know what I mean?"

"I do. I felt that way after my divorce. Jim always made fun of my painting, so I put it aside for a long time. When I finally got it back out, I felt all rusty and out of practice. It's the same thing with dating."

"Ugh. What a horrible word."

"I know. It's the pits. But there are a lot of ways to make it easier. I'm just about due for another party. Give me a weekend you'll be free, and I'll make everyone I invite bring an eligible guy. There's bound to be someone you hit it off with, even if you just go out for a while. You know, like training wheels on a bicycle."

"Yeah. You're right. I just look at everything, and I get scared."

"Take it a step at a time. My old teacher used to say, 'You've got to prime the canvas before you start painting.'"

Alex took another sip of her wine, then turned slightly on the overstuffed striped sofa as she heard the sound of a car coming down the street.

"I think Jesse's home."

"Hmm. I'm gonna run. And I'll ask him if he has any friends—"

"You, Karin, are a peach."

After her friend left, Alex sat quietly on the couch. She clicked off the light and sat in the darkness, enjoying the view from the top of the hill. It had been one of the reasons she'd wanted to buy this house, a view that encompassed the Hollywood sign, Griffith Park Observatory and then swept all the way downtown to the Wilshire district. At night, bright lights sparkling, you saw Los Angeles at her sultry, colorful best.

She didn't have time to enjoy it. She was rarely home. And when she was, she was usually asleep. Exhausted. Weekends were a mad whirl of shopping, laundry, errands—

Enough. She leaned back into the comfort of the sofa and took another sip of white wine. *After the wedding, it's time for you to start living your life. Three months from now, things have simply got to change.*

"YES, MRS. BRADFORD, I understand you want a Renaissance theme. But are you sure you want to go with authentic food? I think it might be...awfully heavy this time of year. Perhaps Pierre could come up with something a little more *nouvelle*—"

Alex had dealt with the Constance Bradfords of the world before. The women who walked into her office and sought her professional advice as a caterer smelled of money. Designer dresses. The finest leathers. Real gemstones. And they usually pulled up to the hotel in one of their Rolls-Royces.

Yet none of this had ever intimidated Alex. She had grown up with money, then decided she wanted to make it on her own terms. An only child, she had always been independent.

"No, I want everything to be as authentic as possible." Constance's china-blue eyes were regal and cool. "Now, did you check into getting the pheasants?"

Alex lowered her gaze to the page in front of her. As long as she had been in catering, some things never ceased to amaze her. This woman wanted several braces of pheasants, costing a *ton* of money, to be carried in at the head of a processional. What a way to begin a wedding. But then again, it was never wise to question the decisions of the very rich—if you wanted their business.

"Yes. That's all taken care of. And I checked about costuming the waiters. The ice sculptures have been ordered. Now, about the flowers—"

"All white. And nothing ordinary. I don't want roses or carnations or any of that—"

"I know just the man. He did Jessica Jamison's wedding last year, and everyone talked about those flowers for months—"

"Yes." Constance's eyes were admiring as she studied Alex. Alex looked back at her, her expression serene. "Yes, that will do quite nicely. Only I want more flowers than at Jessica's wedding, masses of flowers—"

"David's your man."

As Constance checked over other details, Alex glanced covertly at the bride-to-be. Elizabeth "Muffy" Bradford, youngest child and only daughter of the Bradford dynasty. She was a pale little thing and looked nervous.

Who wouldn't be, with that mother of hers.

Bloodless. That was the word. The diamond on the third finger of her left hand was enormous. Ostentatious. Her fingers were so tiny, and Alex knew she wasn't imagining the slight tremor. Even in designer clothing, she had an air about her that suggested a little girl who was uncomfortable in her Sunday-school dress.

Constance's makeup was flawless. She looked like an ad for Estée Lauder. Muffy's light pink lipstick was slightly smeared, as if she were a little girl playing at her mother's dressing table.

To have a mother who was so incredibly icy and seemed utterly perfect was not Alex's idea of a good time. She'd noticed that Muffy, in the short time she'd been in the office with Constance, was not at all like a normal bride-to-be. Most of them were excited, overflowing with plans for their special day. Muffy just sat in her chair. Lifeless. Fragile.

Alex, who usually had excellent instincts about people, couldn't figure Muffy out. Not just yet.

She simply felt sorry for her.

"Muffy, what do you think of that?" This, from Constance.

"Yes, that sounds fine." The soft, restrained voice. The gentle nodding of the head, the swing of blunt-cut chin-length hair against her delicate jaw. And the absolutely vacant expression in her eyes.

As if she were dreaming...

But Alex didn't have any more time that day to wonder about Muffy Bradford and her mother. Constance kept her on her toes for the rest of the meeting, and then she had an Iranian mother and daughter coming in, then a bat mitzvah, and after that... Another typical day at the Biltmore. And a very long one.

SEAN LAWTON GAZED around the Bradfords' formal dining room with carefully concealed distaste. He had grown up with money and had made even more. He knew the sort of power it gave a person.

You could tell a lot about someone just by seeing what money did to them.

Money didn't change people. It simply amplified qualities already present. In the case of the Bradford family, it amplified unhappiness—for everyone except Constance.

He felt Muffy looking at him before he turned toward her and saw her frightened, pale blue gaze. They were sitting next to each other, across from another couple Constance had invited to dinner. Sean kept his eyes on Muffy's wan face as he took her hand in his. Her fingers were cold. Small and fragile. He rubbed her hand gently, hoping to transfer some of his warmth to her.

Bloodless, he thought suddenly. Then, realizing it wasn't Muffy he was thinking of, he turned his attention to the woman at the end of the table.

Constance Bradford. Impeccably dressed in something blue and silk and simple. He didn't have a head for designer labels, but he was sure whatever Constance put on her perfectly toned, manicured and pedicured body had someone's signature on it.

She was watching them, a slight smile on her perfectly glossed lips.

He smiled back, holding her eyes with his until it became a silent challenge. He was gratified when she looked away, but sure she knew exactly what she was doing by deferring to him.

Phillip, I feel sorry for you. You're going to have your hands full with that one.

He hadn't really understood his best friend's decision, at first. When Phillip asked Sean to meet for a drink after work only a few weeks ago, he'd had no idea what his friend was up to. Until several glasses of fine Scotch had given him some Dutch courage.

"I love Muffy, and I don't know what to do about that mother of hers," Phillip confessed, running his slender, artistic fingers through his thick blond hair.

"Run off with Muffy, that's the best way," Sean had advised.

Phillip turned bloodshot, anguished eyes in the direction of his friend. "You don't understand. Muffy—God, Sean, I love her, but she doesn't seem capable of standing up to her mother. I was invited to dinner the other night, and Constance made it quite clear I wasn't good enough for her daughter and was not to come around again."

"The only reason that you're not good enough for her precious Muffy," Sean said carefully, "is that you've declined going into the family business. Believe me, if that woman knew you'd inherit all your father's money, she'd find a way to get rid of her own husband." He carefully finished his drink. Normally, he wasn't a man to overindulge, but tonight, whenever his glass was half empty, Phillip insisted on filling it again.

"That won't happen. I've fought with Father enough." Phillip gazed morosely at his empty glass, then looked at Sean's, half full. Reaching for the bottle of Scotch, he tipped it toward Sean's glass, but was forestalled by Sean's hand covering the top of the crystal tumbler.

"I've had enough. I'll have to call Brian as it is and ask him to pick me up. I wouldn't want to be on the road in this condition."

Phillip smiled, then refilled his own glass. "We've had some good times, haven't we, Sean?"

"That we have."

"Remember the time we were in that bar in— What was the name of that country?"

Sean had to smile. "The time that man threw his chair at me?"

Phillip laughed, the soft light in his office burnishing his hair. "And all over that girl, the one selling shells on the beach. I knew we were in for it the minute she looked at you."

Sean nodded, smiling as he stared at his glass. "Couldn't have gotten out of that one if you hadn't thought as quickly as you did."

"Well, there's no way on earth that sod would have attacked a priest."

"Father Lawton." Sean started to laugh, then leaned back in his chair, the tumbler in his hands. "My God, the times we've had."

"You've always been there for me, Sean." There was a peculiar intensity in Phillip's voice, and if Sean hadn't been so besotted, he would have picked up on it.

"As you've been for me."

Phillip took a last mouthful of Scotch, swallowed it, then set down the empty glass. "I wonder if you could see to helping me out one last time."

Sean eyed his friend, frown lines appearing in his forehead. "Sounds serious."

"It is." Quickly Phillip outlined his plan as Sean listened as carefully as he was able.

"All you have to do is stand in for me. Convince Constance that you want to marry Muffy and let her wallow around in all the wedding preparations. She likes you, Sean, I have no doubt she'd try to marry you herself if she thought the old man would stand for it."

"Not me." Sean grinned. "The money. She'd like to roll around in my money. God knows we've both seen enough of that type." And he'd remembered the time Constance had cornered him at a party and the message that had been coolly apparent in her eyes.

"Then, at the last minute, when the minister is reading the final vows, I'll jump in from the side and, before the old witch knows what hit her, Muffy and I will be man and wife."

The idea had its own peculiar type of charm. Sean pictured her serene highness, the venerable Mrs. Constance Bradford, apoplectic with rage. He grinned.

"I'll do it. One last thing, though. Why me? There are a score of other men you could have asked, and all of them would have been eager to pull this over on Constance."

Phillip leaned forward, a lock of tousled blond hair spilling over his high forehead. "I trust you. I love Muffy with my life, Sean. If this goes wrong, her mother will send her away, keep us apart for the rest of our lives. I think, even now, Constance may suspect something.

"I've watched her for years, seen what she's done—I know what she could do to Muffy. I love Muffy, and I want to spend the rest of my life making her happy and protecting her from that old battle-ax."

Sean finished his drink, then leaned back and gazed at his friend. "You're a lucky man."

Phillip eyed his friend, then a slow grin crossed his face. "I'll be damned. And to think I bought that bull about living a life on the edge, never settling down, making each day a grand adventure."

"You keep my secret, I'll keep yours."

"You're a bigger romantic than I am! Good God, Sean, what's holding up your getting married?"

"If," Sean said slowly, looking intently at the tumbler in his hands sparkling in the soft lamplight, "I could find a woman who wasn't so damned intent on my money and had some feeling strictly for me—"

"You'd marry her in a second!"

Sean slowly nodded his head, then set the glass down on Phillip's desk. "But, as I don't see that happening, I'll simply continue on my merry way."

"It happens, Sean. When you least expect it." Phillip took a deep breath. "Muffy told me that if we had to disappear and go live on some desert island, she'd do it."

"Treasure that, Phil. Hell, treasure *her.*"

"Then you'll help us?"

Sean stood up and walked slowly over to the office window. Phillip had started his own advertising firm with a trust fund from his grandmother, and his office had a spectacular view of downtown Los Angeles. It was a clear night, and he gazed out over the miles of twinkling lights.

"If I believed in true love—for myself, I mean—and up to now I've had no reason to—" He stopped, then turned toward his friend, his hands in his pockets and a slightly vulnerable smile on his face.

"Hell, Phil. I can try to imagine how much this means to you. I'm all yours."

Muffy's fingers gently squeezing his brought Sean out of his thoughts. He looked down at her, a slightly puzzled expression on his face.

"Mother wanted to know how your latest deal was coming along."

Her voice was soft, almost childlike. Dressed in a strapless evening gown that looked far too old for her, Muffy smiled up at him. And Sean had to admire her courage. Sheltered and bullied all her young life, this entire scheme was requiring all the courage the fragile girl had.

Phillip was a lucky man.

And a good friend. Sean had agreed to participate in the deception in order to help the young couple get out from underneath Constance's domination, her carefully calculated machinations. Sean didn't even think Phillip himself had any idea how nasty this woman could get if she were pushed to the wall.

She certainly wouldn't be pleased to know her only daughter was determined to marry for love.

It was up to him to help them pull this entire thing off, and he hadn't hesitated. Phillip had always been there for him in the past, and Sean believed in loyalty toward the few people he was close to. Phil was entrusting him with his future, and Sean was determined to do everything he could to see to it that Muffy and Phillip succeeded.

The room seemed uncomfortably warm. He'd stay just as long as he had to, then make a graceful exit. And on to the Biltmore.

Alexandra Michaels. The woman who was in charge of this "Wedding of the Year," as the press had dubbed it. He had to check her out, see if there were going to be any complications on that end. He knew she was a hard worker, and would still be in her office later this evening.

Once he had her all figured out, saw where she fit into this master plan, then all he had to do was wait for the big day.

Simple. As easy and uncomplicated as any one of the deals he made every day.

And, of course, he'd have to keep Constance in a state of happy anticipation over the thought of getting her manicured, pampered hands on his money.

He turned to face Constance Bradford, knowing the deal she was feigning interest in didn't excite her half as much as the prospect of his making piles of money.

They're all the same in the end. Every last one of them.

He could believe in luck for his friend. But not for himself. If there was a woman out there who wanted him and not his money, he had yet to find her.

"I'M LEAVING, ALEX. See you tomorrow."

Alex glanced up at Marcy, her personal assistant. Sometimes she secretly envied the woman. Marcy, a petite redhead with amazing curly hair and a dancer's figure, had one of the most interesting lives in the office. Her job was a job, of the nine-to-five-bring-in-the-money variety.

Her real life began when she left the office, always in a variety of stunning, stylish outfits. The last thing Alex had heard was that she had been at a friend's party and taken up with a Russian dancer who was in town on an extended tour.

Marcy always looked happy. Radiant. Fulfilled.

You are losing your mind. Alex pushed herself away from her desk and stretched. Then she tucked her silk blouse back into the waistband of her skirt. The matching jacket was draped over her chair. This late at night, alone in the office, she felt she could relax just a little. Her pumps had been replaced by slippers. Her hair, usually confined in an elegant twist, had been released and now spilled down her back.

It was her one concession to femininity. Her hair reached the small of her back, and Alex had never thought of cutting it. There were certain things she couldn't give up.

She walked over to the window, her steps muffled by the thick, cream carpeting. The catering offices were finally in order, after what seemed like months of working in small closets or rooms with walls torn down or plastered. Now, the remodeled offices Alex slipped in and out of were as luxurious as the rest of the old hotel.

It was starting to rain again. Having lived in Los Angeles all her life, Alex could never understand it when people insisted there were no changes in weather when one lived in the City of Angels. They were there, just more subtle. You had to know what to look for.

The only light in the office came from the lamp on her desk, casting a small circle of illumination and leaving the rest of the room in shadows.

She leaned against the heavy plate glass and watched the rain make sparkling rivulets down the surface of the window. And she realized that, in a manner that was usual for her, she was feeling decidedly sorry for herself.

Leave it alone. You're just overtired. You let old Bulldozer Bradford get to you.

But it was more than that. Leaving for work this morning, she had seen Karin kissing Jesse goodbye. They had been totally engrossed in each other, had barely noticed her as she walked to her Mercedes. Then Marcy, this afternoon during her lunch break, had been whispering wild weekend plans over the phone to her Russian. Even Pierre, whose love life was a constant source of office gossip, was spending the weekend in Palm Springs with a new love.

Everyone has someone but you.

She felt as vulnerable as a grade-school girl without a single valentine. The job, the house, the money and status—it wasn't enough.

In the long run, by itself, it didn't add up to much of anything.

Arms crossed in front of her, Alex rubbed her palms up and down her upper arms. The office seemed cold. Probably the rain. She'd have to remember to turn on her electric blanket before she got into bed.

She was surprised to find tears pricking behind her eyes. For the fleetest of seconds, the view below blurred even more, but then Alex blinked the tears away and took a deep breath.

I wish... Oh, I wish...

"Miss Michaels?"

The deep, masculine voice caused a delicious little tremor, a shivering up the spine. Alex turned and saw a tall silhouette in her doorway.

"Alexandra Michaels?" That voice again.

She cleared her throat, certain if she didn't her voice would tremble. "Yes? Can I help you with anything?"

She wasn't afraid. There were still plenty of people on the floor, and this man didn't inspire that sort of fear. It was something different, something much more elusive. Alex swallowed, then walked slowly toward her desk and the light.

He advanced at the same time, and it seemed to Alex, as the light caught his face and brought it into her vision, that he was the most stunningly handsome man she had seen in years. Thick, dark hair shot with the slightest silver strands. Blue-gray, penetrating eyes. Strong jaw, broad shoulders, a solid body. She'd bet there wasn't any fat beneath that Armani suit.

He was simply devastating.

"I wanted—" He stopped speaking and simply looked at her. Alex couldn't seem to glance away. Her heart was starting to race, her blood seemed to be thrumming throughout her body. Everything was a little brighter, her body seemed more sensitive.

She couldn't stop looking at him.

He finally had the grace to look away, and once he did, Alex quickly sat down at her desk. She couldn't explain it, but she felt the need to put something, *anything*, between her and this man. Determined not to be caught gawking again, she glanced up at him quickly and motioned him into a chair.

He sat down, then leaned forward. Alex looked up and found he was studying her again. She flushed as she realized the picture she presented and quickly slipped out of her scuffs, her stockinged feet searching for her pumps. At the same time, she reached for her hair with one hand and for the small stack of pins on her desk with the other.

"Leave it."

Her hands stilled their frantic motion.

"Leave it down. It's quite becoming."

"I'm glad you think so." The words slipped out of her mouth so easily she thought she'd imagined saying them. But as she saw the warmth and—what?—male, animal *heat* come into his eyes, she realized she'd spoken them out loud.

This is not like you, Alex. Not at all.

But as the thought flashed through her mind, Alex rejected it. It had been much too long since she'd met a man like this. She'd been working too many impossible hours, driving home to an empty house every night. She was long overdue for a chance to spend some time talking with an immensely attractive man.

Let alone anything else.

Her mind was going into overdrive. Could one's libido hyperventilate?

Enjoy this, a lively little voice in the back of her mind was whispering. *There's something going on here, something absolutely delicious.*

She slowly lowered her arms and placed her hands in front of her on the desktop. Her eyes never left his face, and his expression was appreciative.

"So, what is it exactly that you want?" She knew her cheeks were slightly flushed, her eyes dancing. He was fabulous. She'd glanced quickly at his left hand when he'd entered the small circle of light, and there wasn't a ring on his finger. And the energy in her office, the way he was looking at her—he definitely liked women.

He hesitated for just an instant, then said quietly, "I wanted to discuss the Bradford wedding."

She picked up the sudden change in the air instantly, but didn't look away. She hadn't become head of catering by standing on the sidelines.

"What exactly did you want to discuss?"

He seemed angry suddenly, glancing away from her, his penetrating gaze sweeping her dimly lit office. As if he were trying to find out more about her by looking at where she worked.

Lived, Alex corrected herself silently.

But he wasn't angry with her. There was a sense of pent-up frustration, of something beyond his control. And Alex had the feeling that this was a man who lived life on his own terms, who was in total control most of the time.

"Is everything going smoothly?" Now his voice was soft, his gaze back on her.

Alex met his gaze head on. "Yes, it is. Everything's right on schedule."

"Is Constance giving you a hard time?"

Alex felt her eyes narrow before she had a chance to keep her expression smooth and unreadable. Was this man one of Constance's little henchmen trying to catch her unaware? Other women had tried similar tricks, not trusting her to orchestrate one of the most important days of their lives.

She rejected the thought immediately. This man danced to no one's tune but his own.

"No. She knows what she wants, and it's my business to give it to her."

"And Muffy? How is she holding up?"

Alex chose her words carefully. "I have to believe she's getting exactly what she wants, as well."

His eyes were full of admiration, and Alex had the strangest feeling that what they were saying had not the slightest relation to what was really going on. She dropped her gaze to his hands. Strong hands, tanned, with a sprinkling of dark hair. Masterful hands...

Her mind started to wander, with visions of the two of them alone, the door locked, the backs of her thighs pressed up against the hard wood of her desk as he slid his hands up beneath her skirt, bent her back and—

She snapped her mind back to the present and had the uncanniest feeling he'd known exactly what she was thinking—or suspected something similar.

"Was there anything else—" She stopped and cleared her throat. It was tight, all of a sudden. She swallowed. "Was there anything else you wanted, Mr.—"

Was it her imagination, or were his eyes regretful?

"Sean. Sean Lawton."

"Mr. Lawton. Was there anything—"

She stopped. Frozen. Staring at him.

Fate was playing one of her nastier varieties of practical jokes. Alex sat back in her seat and stared at him.

This couldn't possibly be happening.

He'd walked into her office, and she'd lit up like a Christmas tree. What was it Karin had said? *You need to get your valves blown out.*

"Alexandra—"

"Don't." Her instincts were screaming at her, she knew what he wanted to say, and she couldn't bear to have it put into words. Alex held up her hand, as if to physically ward him off.

—your eggs fried—

"We have to talk—"

"No, we don't." Her voice was resolutely bright.

You need to find a man who charges your battery, stokes your fire—I'm talking passion with a capital P.

"And if I say you're wrong—"

"No!" Alex stood up, glad to get her face out of the relentless glare of her desk lamp. She grabbed for her suit jacket, shrugged it on, then opened her desk drawer and snatched up her purse. Backing away from her desk, she

gave Sean Lawton a wide berth as she walked swiftly to the door.

"Alexandra—" He was on his feet now.

Even the way he said her name made it sound like a caress.

She didn't turn around until the elevator door closed, then she sagged against the wall and stared at the wild-eyed woman looking back at her.

Sean Lawton had walked into her office and exploded all of her preconceptions about love—*lust,* she corrected herself—at first sight. He'd affected her as violently as a punch to the stomach.

And she was arranging his wedding.

Chapter Two

"—the most incredibly handsome man! And then you look at Muffy, and you wonder why—"

All conversation between the secretaries ceased as Alex swept into the catering office. She hadn't slept well, and there were circles under her eyes that all the concealer in the world couldn't have helped.

The news was out. Sean Lawton was hot office gossip.

Marcy leapt to her feet and followed Alex into her office, a sheaf of memos in her hands. As Alex slipped her purse into a drawer, Marcy stepped up to the side of her desk and waited.

Alex rummaged around in her drawer as she composed herself. She'd had a lot of time to think last night. Her mind had been in such a confused state she hadn't slept at all. And she'd come to a major decision.

Sean Lawton was not going to come between her and her job. Her safe, demanding, everyday routine was the only thing she had in her life that could steady her, protect her. She was going to give him and Muffy the wedding of the year if it killed her.

She'd already asked for vacation time directly after the Bradford wedding, and last night she had decided to take it as far away from Southern California as possible.

It was too bad her travel agent didn't know of any chartered flights to the moon.

"Alex? I need your signature on these."

Alex glanced at the memos, scanned them quickly, then picked up a pen and began to sign them.

"Have you seen him yet?" Marcy was always on top of the hottest office gossip. She was never malicious, but she enjoyed talking about interesting people, and at the Biltmore she had plenty of opportunity to observe some of the best.

"Who?"

"Who else? Sean Lawton. I think he looks like that guy who played James Bond in—"

"Timothy Dalton."

"Yeah. With a little bit of Sean Connery thrown in."

"It's just the dark hair and light eyes. It's a striking combination, I'll admit, but it doesn't do much for me—"

"Ms. Michaels?"

That voice. She was doomed.

Alex glanced up, praying that Sean Lawton hadn't heard what she'd said. Though at this moment, she would have welcomed him getting angry and taking his wedding elsewhere. Anywhere. Away from her.

She and Marcy stared as Sean walked slowly into her office and sat down in one of the leather chairs by her desk. His dark suit fit him perfectly; it had to be custom made. He leaned forward, that same intent look she remembered last night in his eyes, his posture relaxed.

As relaxed as a panther about to spring.

Marcy snapped out of her trance. "Would you like some, ah, coffee? We have tea, too, you know. Or maybe some juice? You know, I could run and get some fresh Danish—"

"Coffee would be fine." Sean smiled at Marcy, and she scooted out. Alex glanced at her departing form, knowing it would be at least ten minutes before anything resembling coffee was brought to her office. Sean Lawton, in the flesh, in her office—Marcy would undoubtedly regale the office with her part in this moment in catering history.

Alex sighed, then turned to face Sean Lawton. The day she'd been assigned the Bradford wedding, she'd gone over the cast of characters carefully. Constance the bulldozer. Muffy the mouse. John Bradford, henpecked husband and brilliant businessman.

And Sean. In his early forties, he had more money than he'd ever spend in his lifetime. Slowly, ever so slowly, he was redesigning the Los Angeles skyline. Lawton Towers. Lawton Place. Every time you picked up the paper, he was in it, in either the society pages or the business section. He had an incredible lineup of beautiful female escorts, but Alex had never seen a picture of him with Muffy.

Maybe it had been a quick romance. Passionate.

Muffy, passionate? The two words didn't belong in the same sentence.

Sean Lawton belonged to that small group of men one fantasized about. He lived a life straight out of a nighttime soap, moved among the richest and most powerful people on the planet.

And he made her feel as if she were going through an early menopause, heavy on the hot flashes.

Alex smiled, deciding the best defense was a good offense.

"So, Mr. Lawton, was the Renaissance theme your idea?"

The expression on his face confirmed her suspicions. Constance Bulldozer Bradford was in charge of this little party. It surprised Alex. She would have thought Sean able to handle the woman.

"I guess not," she replied softly.

He was simply staring at her. Sizing her up. Making her nervous.

"Mr. Lawton, unless you have something you'd like to say, I suggest—"

She never finished her sentence. The door to her office burst in, and Pierre came charging in, carrying a tray in his hands.

"Alex, my darling, you have to taste this! They didn't have this exact recipe during the Renaissance, but we don't have to let Mrs. Bradford know—"

"What is it, Pierre?" Now she was getting annoyed. Sean was sitting back comfortably in his seat, smiling. He was amused.

"My idea for the cake. Most wedding cake is—how do you say?—dry. Tasteless. Terrible. This, *this* little cake will become the talk of the catering world."

Alex had to smile. She loved passion in her co-workers, and Pierre was passionate about his cooking. A tall, rangy man with sandy blond curls and twinkling blue eyes, Pierre was the consummate temperamental Frenchman. But everyone in the catering offices adored him.

He'd made Alex his special pet because she really appreciated his food and told him so. Thus, she was the first to sample any of his culinary triumphs or disasters.

Pierre set the tray down on her desk. There was a large slice of chocolate cake on a delicate china plate, and a silver fork.

"Tell me the truth," Pierre said quietly. Then, as if noticing Sean for the first time, he said, "Alex, she always tells me the truth. There are not many people with that quality, don't you agree?"

Sean nodded his head and watched as Alex brought the forkful of cake closer to her mouth.

She could barely swallow, she was so nervous. But she managed to maneuver the fork to her mouth without making a mess of it, even though her hand was trembling the slightest bit.

The cake melted in her mouth. Rich, dark chocolate. Raspberries. And something else. It was always the "something else" that set Pierre's cooking apart from the rest of the catering world.

"It's wonderful."

Pierre smiled, then kissed his fingers. "For you, Alex." He turned to Sean. "She's the best. Always working, working, working. I asked her to come to Palm Springs with me this weekend. Even the hardest workers need a vacation now and then, don't you agree, Mr—"

"Lawton. But call me Sean."

Pierre's eyes widened, and he looked guiltily at Alex. "Forgive me, *ma chère,* I thought he was a friend of yours, not a client."

"Why don't *you* try the cake, Mr. Lawton? After all, it is your wedding." She was pleased with herself, her tone pure professional.

"Cut me a piece," he replied.

Pierre seemed fascinated as Alex took the same fork she'd used and sliced through the delicate cake. She leaned forward at the same time Sean did and started as he grasped her wrist and guided the fork toward his mouth.

His touch was everything she'd thought it would be. Warm. Firm. Assured.

Sean didn't even pause to think after he sampled the cake. "Wonderful, Pierre. I think it will be a wedding the guests will never forget."

He was still holding her wrist, and Alex gently but firmly pulled her hand away from his grasp. She turned to find Pierre looking at both of them with an amused expression.

"So, *ma coeur,* I will add that cake to the menu, no?"

"Yes. As long as Mr. Lawton has approved it, I doubt if Mrs. Bradford will challenge the decision."

Taking one last look at the two of them, Pierre turned and walked slowly out of the office. Alex frowned. Unusual. Pierre usually raced out of her office. He never seemed to move at a regular pace, his volatile mind was always a step ahead of where he was.

"Now, Mr. Lawton—"

"I've got the coffee." Marcy appeared in the doorway, balancing a huge tray. Alex usually got her own coffee, and she never brought in Danish or muffins because Pierre usually had something for her to try. But Marcy had piled the tray with a bowl of fresh fruit and assorted baked treats.

Sean Lawton was making everyone behave in an out-of-the-ordinary way. Maybe he had the same effect on everyone and she should take no notice of the way he made her feel. It would be like trying to fence in a tidal wave.

Alex bit her lip as she watched Marcy carefully set the tray down on a corner of her large desk.

He's still a client. Treat him with respect. Alex picked up the silver coffeepot and poured Sean a cup, then passed it to him.

"Danish?" she asked, trying for a tone she usually heard only on *Masterpiece Theater*.

"Maybe that blueberry one."

She handed him the Danish and a napkin, then poured herself a cup of coffee and added cream and sugar.

Now, perhaps they would get some privacy and he would be able to tell her why he was in her office.

But he simply sat there, quietly eating his Danish and drinking his coffee.

What is this, some kind of game to annoy me? Alex decided she would find refuge in her role as I-am-caterer-hear-me-roar.

"What is it exactly that you want to talk about, Mr. Lawton?"

"Sean. Please."

She'd thought about his name last night, about how easy it was to say, how it had felt coming out of her mouth. Now she knew she couldn't refuse him this small request without coming off as incredibly petty.

"Sean." She took another sip of her coffee. One of the perks of her job was that the Biltmore served some of the best coffee in the world. It sure beat anything she could make.

"I did some checking up on you last night," he began.

She could feel herself starting to bristle.

"I was curious, Alexandra—"

"Alex. Call me Alex." No one had called her Alexandra for years, and the way this man made her name sound was the equivalent of what Mel Gibson did for black leather in *The Road Warrior*. Having him call her Alex was much safer.

He eyed her for just a second longer, then softly said, "Alex it is. Don't be offended at what I did."

"I'm just curious as to why."

"I have my reasons. There are a few things I'd like you to do for me."

Unbidden, the thoughts she'd had about the two of them and her desk flashed through her mind. Alex pushed them away, took another sip of coffee.

"What did you have in mind?"

He set his cup of coffee down on the desk, leaned forward and looked directly into her eyes. Alex briefly registered that he hadn't gotten a crumb of Danish, not a speck of powdered sugar, on that dark gray suit. Some things in life just weren't fair.

"I'd like you to help me give three parties before the wedding. I have an enormous amount of people I need to entertain. I'd thought of simply catering the parties out of my home, but it would be so much more convenient for me to have them here."

She thought about what would happen if she accepted. More contact with Sean. Seeing him with Muffy. Having to fight this ridiculous attraction.

She thought about what would happen if she refused. The wedding of the year would probably go straight down the toilet.

Alex had her pride. Even if her personal life had never been something to phone home about—especially with her mother's attitude—she still took pride in the life she'd built for herself, in the work she did.

She glanced at the marble-and-chrome clock on her desk. "My next appointment is in twenty minutes. Why don't you give me a brief outline of what it is you'd like and on what evenings?"

Fifteen minutes later, Sean stood. Alex followed his lead and tried not to let him see how his handshake affected her. She watched him as he walked slowly out of her office, his movements self-assured and relaxed.

He was almost out the door when an obvious oversight occurred to her.

"Sean!"

He stopped, turned around and stared at her.

Alex flushed slightly, feeling the telltale pinpricks of heat rising in her cheeks. "How do I reach you if I need to talk to you?"

His smile was slow. Confident. Something about the way he was looking at her made Alex grasp the back of her chair for additional support.

"I've made it easy for you, Alex. You just have to buzz me. I'll be staying in the Presidential Suite until the day of the wedding."

The Presidential Suite. The top two floors of this hotel. He's going to be around constantly. This cannot be happening to me.

And, having dropped that little bomb, Sean Lawton slowly sauntered out the door.

"ALEX? ARE YOU all right?"

Marcy's concerned voice made Alex glance away from the window and toward the doorway. Marcy, purse in hand, was getting ready to leave for the day.

"I'm fine." She decided to make an effort. "So where are you going tonight?"

"Where else? The ballet." She fiddled with the strap on her purse, then reached up and pushed her thick, reddish curls off her forehead. "Look, Alex, I know I acted like sort of a goon today—"

"Don't worry about it."

"But that guy—I mean, Alex, *Peter* doesn't even affect me that way! And it wasn't just me, everyone in the office was swooning. And then, when we heard that he's going to be *living* here for the next few months—"

"I'm sure it's just so that he can be right on top of things." *Literally.* "If we can pull off this Renaissance extravaganza, we'll be way ahead of the other hotels in the city."

Marcy just stared at her for a moment, then said quietly, "Louise was right."

Alex was all attention now. Louise Hartson was one of the caterers who worked under her direction. And she wasn't one of Alex's favorite people. Other people simply had flat tires when they were late coming into work. Louise was almost killed when her tire exploded and practically had to call out the National Guard. Most people quietly broke their nails and fixed them at their desks. Not Louise. If she broke a nail, lost the heel of one of her shoes, spilled some coffee on her skirt—it could quickly reach catastrophic proportions.

There was a streak of maliciousness in Louise when she wasn't looking for attention or basking in reflected glory. Alex was constantly picking up the pieces of her catering projects, and just last week had seriously considered firing the woman.

Louise was the consummate California beach girl, getting a little older but still holding up well. Her tan was perfect, her streaked hair artful, her outfits barely professional by Biltmore standards.

And if Louise thought there was anything going on between Alex and Sean Lawton—even if all the action was only in Alex's mind—it would be a total, unmitigated disaster.

"Right about what?"

Marcy looked miserable, and Alex realized she hadn't intended to say the words out loud. But Alex couldn't back away now. She knew that whatever Louise had had to say, it couldn't be that good.

"Right about what?" she repeated.

"Oh, Alex, I don't want you to think that all I do out there is sit and gossip—"

"I know that's not true. Now tell me what Louise said."

"She said—she said it was true what everyone had suspected all along, that you had ice water for blood if Sean Lawton couldn't get a rise out of you."

Alex smiled. If she had Louise fooled, she had the entire office fooled. Now she had to make sure that extended to Mr. Lawton himself.

"I'm sorry, Alex."

"Don't be. You can't control what comes out of that woman's mouth. And you know she likes to talk about everyone. If not me, someone else."

"You're not upset?"

"Marcy, if I let myself get upset at everything Louise said, I'd be a candidate for early retirement. The woman's a pest, nothing more or less."

"She's not doing real well with the Farrell wedding."

"Tell me something I don't know."

Marcy smiled. "Okay. Thanks, Alex. I'll see you tomorrow."

Once she was alone in the office, Alex sat back in her chair and closed her eyes. *Ice water for blood.* Louise could be mean, but she'd never made this personal an attack. And saying it in front of Marcy when she knew it would get back to Alex... Louise had to know how close she'd come to getting fired, and she probably resented it.

But if Alex had fired Louise last week, that would have meant taking on three more weddings and a bat mitzvah on top of the Bradford Renaissance Faire. It would have been impossible.

If Louise can only hang in for a couple of months...

"ALEX? ARE YOU all right?"

She opened her eyes and glanced quickly toward the door. Sean stood there, leaning against the door frame, a look of concern in his eyes.

There was something different about him. As the thought flicked through her mind, Alex realized he wasn't wearing a suit. Sean looked entirely different in faded jeans and a black pullover sweater.

"I'm fine." She slid open the drawer of her desk and reached for her purse, averting her eyes. She didn't want to look at him; she didn't even want to acknowledge his existence.

"You look tired."

"It's been a long day. You know all about those."

"Have dinner with me."

She had to admire him; he was direct. And after years of laid-back California men whose attitude reeked of, "Hey, babe, I'm great. Come on to me," Sean's approach was a refreshing change.

"I'm having dinner with some friends."

"Tomorrow night."

If he wanted a challenge, he'd get one. "Sean, I don't know what you hope to accomplish with these dinner invitations, but I want you to know I'm getting the feeling what you have in mind has nothing to do with business.''

Silence.

She decided to plunge ahead.

"Now, correct me if I'm wrong, but you're a man who's engaged to be married, and I just happen to be putting together that wedding. I know men generally get nervous before the big day and perhaps contemplate having a few flings. But I want to get one thing straight—I'm nobody's fling. Got it?"

She could be as direct as he could. She'd expected annoyance. Even anger. Alex was surprised to see the beginnings of a smile forming around his mouth.

"Was what I said so amusing?"

"No. No, Alex, your feelings are dead on."

She was astonished. She'd expected him to avoid the issue when she'd cornered him; she'd thought he would tell her what she felt was all in her head and had no basis in reality.

He was honest—to a point. Score one for Sean Lawton.

"So, I've made myself perfectly clear?"

He nodded slowly, his eyes never leaving her face. And in the strangest sense, Alex felt as if she had issued him a challenge and he had taken it.

"I'm nobody's fool—and nobody's conquest."

He shut the door and walked slowly into her office. Alex was amazed at how he seemed to dominate the large space. She could imagine him at business meetings, closing deals, dealing with his opponents. The thought almost scared her. Yet she was sure he wouldn't resort to underhanded methods of dealing with people, in either his personal or professional life.

"So, what do you suggest we do?" he said softly.

She stared up at him. He was throwing the ball into her court, letting her make the decision. She studied his expression carefully and could have sworn that for just an instant he looked as confused as she felt.

"About what?"

"About this. Between us."

"This . . . feeling?" She felt horribly self-conscious putting it into words.

"Yes."

Suddenly she felt unbearably tired. A part of her, if she was totally honest with herself, ached at the thought of giving up. She longed to throw caution to the wind and not think of Muffy or the wedding or her mother or her job or anything that got in the way of the primitive reaction she was having to this man.

Her fantasies had always been highly imaginative and extremely entertaining and had served her well during the current dry spell that passed for a sensual life. Last night, staring at the ceiling as Roscoe had snored softly nearby, her fantasies had woven extremely erotic images through her brain and had swiftly moved from her desk to the big bed in the Presidential Suite.

So easy. No one would ever have to know. A few hours, the privacy of a suite, the key turned securely in the lock. A chance to find out what would happen with this man who seemed to be able to ignite her deepest sensuality with a single glance. This type of feeling came along...what, once in a lifetime? The thought seemed so corny, but she knew it was true.

Lust. Pure and simple. Alex wasn't proud of her thoughts, but they were her true thoughts, and she wouldn't push them out of the way. After all, everyone had thoughts like these. It was what one did with them, how a person acted, that mattered.

"It's nothing that can last," she began carefully. "I mean, you must love Muffy if you're going to marry her. What's happening between us—I think I'd label it lust. And lust isn't designed to hold two people together, you know that."

"I disagree," he said quietly.

She couldn't believe what she was hearing.

"I think," he said slowly, "that lust has been the driving force that's kept us from total extinction. I think that when a man wants a woman the way I want you, he goes a little crazy and doesn't think about the repercussions. And that feeling, more than anything, has kept us going, kept mankind alive since the time we crawled up out of the water and decided to make a go of it."

"But we're not crawling now," she countered swiftly. "We stand upright and think things through logically—"

"Bull. You know it's all bull. Tell me this, Alex. You've helped hundreds of people marry for love. And marrying for love alone has only been around for a couple of hundred years. Before that, there were arranged marriages, and people still responded to lust. You and I both know the divorce rate in this country, and I don't think marrying for love alone is that good an idea."

"What is it exactly that you're trying to say?"

"Just that lust has to come into it. I think it's what keeps people together even when life throws them a curve. I think that if the person you're with is someone you're absolutely crazy about—in *lust,* if you want to put it that way—you'll stick it out. And I think feelings that strong don't happen every day, and when they do, they shouldn't be ignored."

He thought like no other man she ever knew, and his logic was giving her a headache. Her fingers clenched into frustrated fists. "What do you want me to do? Tell you that all of this is all right? Just surrender to something that can only last a few months, and then you'll go off and start building a life for yourself with another woman while I come back to work and think about what we had? No thanks. I'd rather be alone. In fact, it's the reason I *have* been alone for over a ye—"

She stopped, then looked down at the carpet. She drew a deep, painful, steadying breath, then locked gazes with Sean once again.

"Don't do this to me. Don't play whatever little game you think you can get away with. I'm not some deal. I'm not a building you can buy and renovate and then cast aside."

"What if I said I thought we could have more than that?"

She could feel the anger starting to bubble inside, growing bigger and bigger until it threatened to break loose and consume her.

"More than what? You mean I could be your little something on the side? I don't think so, Mr. Lawton."

"Sean."

"I think we should go back to a more formal manner of addressing each other."

"Absolutely not."

"You're used to getting your own way, aren't you?"

"I always have."

"Not this time."

"Have you thought, Alex, what we'd be like together? Alone? Have you?"

"I won't deny it. But what you think and what you do—"

"I've always believed in following my instincts."

"Bully for you. And do you always leave disaster in your wake?"

"I'll never hurt you, Alex."

"There's nothing but hurt for me in what you're proposing."

"Trust me."

"*Trust* you! I don't even trust the way I feel about you. And it's lust."

He hadn't touched her, but his eyes were so alive, as if he were burning from within. Alex couldn't tear her gaze away from him.

"You make it sound like something distasteful."

"It frightens me. I don't want to feel this way, Sean."

"Do you think I do? Do you think I wanted things to be this way? If I could have met you at another time, another place—"

"But you didn't. And we have to deal with what we have here and now."

"Alex." He grasped one of her wrists with his fingers and pulled her closer toward him. "Alex, don't run away from me. If I told you I knew there was a way we could work things out—"

"There isn't. Let me go."

"I can't."

And she knew it was true. She was up against him now, and her other hand shot out, fingers splayed against his chest to steady herself. His heartbeat was rapid. She could feel it through the fine wool of his sweater.

His arm was around her waist, pulling her up against him. And though she knew it was crazy, all she could think of was getting closer to this man, touching him, feeling the warmth, the incredible heat of his body. A rush of pure, primal feeling overwhelmed her, and she closed her eyes.

She felt his hands in her hair, taking the pins out and letting the full length cascade down her back. Then he was running his fingers through it, caressing her head, tilting her face up—

She was lost. Somewhere in all of this she must have moved, because she could feel the solid wood of her desk against the back of her thighs, then seconds later he was pressed against her, as close as she wanted him, close enough to make her realize he was as excited as she was.

"Sean?" She didn't recognize her own voice. His name sounded like a plea, as though she was begging him to set her free, to stop these feelings that were racing through her bloodstream and making her body feel so warm and heavy.

A heartbeat later, his mouth covered hers.

And the feelings he'd raised in her, intense, crazy and quixotic, exploded out the top of her head.

He was kissing her as if he were a starving man and he couldn't get enough of her. She was responding, her hands sliding up into his hair, pulling his face down to hers, arching up against him. And it was more than fourteen months of being alone, more than the desire to be close to someone. It felt right. His hands felt as if they had been made to shape her body, his mouth felt right against hers, there was no doubt or hesitation.

She didn't even protest as his hand slid swiftly up from her waist and cupped her breast. His mouth caught her sharp whimper, then she bit his lip as a pleasure so brilliant it was painful shot through her body.

In the back of her mind, she knew she wasn't going to stop him.

Just touching her breast wasn't enough. She felt his impatience as he flicked the buttons of her silk blouse open, then slipped his hand inside. His fingers were warm as they slid over her lacy bra, then moved to the front clasp and did away with the last barrier. When his hand caressed her bare breast, Alex moaned and knew she was lost.

He was kissing her neck now, moving impatiently down her throat, and she sensed a raw, wonderfully male impatience that she knew she was perfectly capable of matching. Had she known this was going to happen, was it why she'd fantasized it? Her head went back, her fingers dug into his shoulders for support as he gently bit the taut skin of her neck.

Don't stop, don't stop—

"Alex?"

She recognized the voice and pulled herself back to reality with a jolt as painful as a bucket of ice water thrown on a sun-warmed body. Alex barely had time to notice Sean blocking her view of the door. All she could see was Louise's face over his shoulder as she stood in the doorway, her hand still on the doorknob.

But that was enough. Her blue eyes were incredulous, then a slow, feline smile spread over her entire face.

"I'm sorry. I didn't know you were—occupied with a client. I'll talk with you in the morning."

She closed the door softly, but Alex kept staring at it. Her body felt numb. If she didn't know better, she'd swear she was going into shock.

Finally, not trusting herself to look at Sean, she forced her fingers to stop trembling as she fastened her bra and began on the buttons of her blouse.

"Alex."

She glanced up and was startled to find he looked as shaken as she felt.

"Alex, I'm sorry."

"It's not your fault. What happened was just as much my—" She tried to think of a suitable word and couldn't come up with one. "Responsibility," she finished tiredly.

What an utterly bland word to describe what had flashed between them.

"Alex, if she hadn't come in—"

"I know."

"I didn't come here tonight with the intention of—"

"I know that. It's all right." She was reaching for her suit jacket, then her purse. Her emotions were on automatic pilot; it was the only way she'd get out of this in one piece.

"Alex, we have to—"

"Talk. I know. But I can't—" Her voice wavered, and she stopped for just an instant, then went on. "I can't tonight. I need to get away from you. Just for a little bit. Just so I can—figure out what I'm going to do. Please, just let me be alone for a while."

He looked as if he wanted to say something, then glanced away, that same angry, frustrated look on his face. Yet Alex was absolutely certain that anger had nothing to do with her.

"I'll talk to you tomorrow, then?"

She nodded her head, too tired to resist.

He stepped closer then, put his hands on her shoulders and gently kissed her forehead.

That kiss was her total undoing. She watched him leave her office, her vision blurring.

When the door shut, she burst into tears.

"KARIN, COULD YOU feed Roscoe for me tonight? I'm going to stay over at the hotel."

There was dead silence on the other end of the line. There was also no love lost between Karin and Roscoe.

"Please? I wouldn't ask if I didn't really need the favor."

"You sound pretty burned out. Okay. It's just that—he scares me a little."

Karin, scared of Roscoe? Alex snuggled back against the pile of pillows on the bed. "He'll be putty in your hands once you open a can of Fancy Feast. Just remember, you're the one with the opposable thumb. He can't open the can by himself."

Karin started to laugh. "Okay."

"I owe you one."

"Just get some sleep. You sound terrible."

Alex hung up the phone and stretched out on the bed. She'd been in this particular hotel room before, on nights when she'd had to work late and be in the office early the next day. It wasn't an unusual occurrence, so she had quite a stash of clothes, cosmetics and personal items squirreled away in her office.

Now, a room-service dinner sitting untouched by the table at the window, the television on with no sound, Alex lay back on the bed and tried to make sense of what had happened in her office.

None of this was normal for her. She wasn't the sort of woman to rush in and create her own adventures. That was more up Karin's line. She wasn't daring; she didn't take risks; she always had to know the rules before she played any game.

Alex had to grin, remembering something her mother had once told her. Meredith Michaels had made arrangements for her daughter to go to an exclusive girls' day camp for two weeks one summer. There were all sorts of sports and activities, but Alex had solemnly told her mother she couldn't possibly attend unless she had a soccer rule book. What if one of the girls there wanted to start a game and she didn't know the rules?

It was a handicap of enormous proportions to the seven-year-old she had been.

At thirty-seven, she could still identify with the child she had been. Here she'd spent the better part of the evening trying to figure out the rules of the game. Only there weren't any rules, there wasn't any way she could get through this in her head using simple logic, the left side of the brain, whatever you wanted to call it.

She was exploring unchartered territory, territory she usually left alone. And she was terrified.

And also exhilarated.

Alex closed her eyes. *If you're totally honest with yourself, it was the most exciting moment of your life. Until Louise walked in. But up to that point, you never felt so alive...*

The depth of her response had shocked her. Her willingness to let Sean do whatever he'd wanted, move as fast as he desired—the only possible explanation was that she'd wanted it, too. She'd felt so right, so alive, so whole in his arms. It was as if her life had suddenly come full circle and the passion she'd always reserved for work had now manifested itself in this incredible man.

Muffy and Sean. That was the ultimate puzzle. Something just didn't click. Or was it that she didn't want it to click? Her mind had been at odds with the relationship from the start. Muffy looked like a good stiff breeze would blow her away. Sean was a man whose passion would be akin to a tornado.

Muffy wouldn't stand a chance.

What did he see in her?

Maybe the obvious. Maybe just the Bradford millions, a dynasty he could have complete control over once her parents kicked off. Maybe Sean was just callous enough that that was all that mattered to him.

Maybe, instead of closing his eyes and thinking of God and country, he closed his eyes and thought of the money he was going to make. Maybe that was what excited him most.

But even as she thought the words, she knew they couldn't be true. Working at the Biltmore had honed her people skills to a razor's edge. She'd always been curious about people, wanting to know all about their lives, what made them happy, what made them sad. What got them crazy. Over the years, as she'd slowly worked her way up the corporate ladder, one of the things that had separated her from the pack had been an uncanny ability to see beyond superficialities and into what the real motivations were.

An Iranian mother was bitchy and nervous because she wanted her daughter to have the wedding she'd never had. A nervous, single father handling his son's bar mitzvah wasn't sure he was up to the job. Even the rich and famous, with their limos, furs and outrageous demands, were just the same when it came to making that final commitment and saying those vows.

Even Constance Bradford— Well, maybe old Bulldozer Bradford was the mighty exception to the rule.

People weren't all that different, money or not. And Alex's ability had spread through word of mouth. People attended her weddings and, impressed, referred business to her.

She treated people like people, and that was why she was so successful.

Muffy. The girl—*woman,* she corrected herself. No, *girl* was really the operative word here. The girl looked like she wasn't even on the planet half the time. She seemed totally indifferent to all the wedding preparations. She looked untouched, innocent—out to lunch.

If I were getting married to Sean, I wouldn't be all that calm. How could any woman be? Look at the effect he'd had on the women in her office. Like catnip. And it was especially potent because he wasn't a man who flaunted his success or his looks or his power.

He was simply himself, and that was more than enough.

What to do. Alex, who planned her way through life and never left home or office without at least a dozen lists, had no idea. Here she was, to all eyes successful and capable, and inside she felt like she was eighteen years old and walking a tightrope.

She glanced at the bedside clock. Three twenty-three. And she had to be in the office at seven, for the monthly meeting.

The monthly meeting. Louise.

Yet as she closed her eyes and tried vainly to drift off to sleep, Alex had to grin.

Ice water in my veins? Don't you wish.

Chapter Three

Sean Lawton stood in one corner of the Biltmore's luxurious Presidential Suite and stared out at the downtown Los Angeles skyline. The sun was just beginning to come up, washing the facades of the tall buildings with a soft, golden light. Another day. And exactly seventy-eight days until the wedding.

Seventy-eight days until he could come clean with Alex, explain the entire mess and give himself a chance to find out if there could be anything more between them than this incredible attraction.

He'd thought of calling Phillip. Sean was positive he could trust Alex with the truth about this wedding. He was merely acting as a stand-in. But he couldn't, because he couldn't reach Phillip.

The trouble with this entire scheme was that he hadn't anticipated meeting Alexandra Michaels.

He wanted to believe she was different, and her background seemed to prove she was. He'd had her checked out, because after that first meeting, he'd realized his emotions were flaring dangerously out of control. And he was a man who had learned early in life the value of staying in control at all times.

What he'd found out had pleased him immensely.

The daughter of James Edward Michaels, and his only child, Alex had turned her back on her family fortune after graduating from a Swiss boarding school. She'd taken some college classes, both here and abroad, and had worked part-time at the Marriott down by LAX. While employed there as a cocktail waitress and later a bartender, she'd fallen into the world of hotel management.

She'd eventually finished her degree—in psychology, with a business minor—then slowly worked her way up the corporate ladder, moving from hotel to hotel as different job opportunities presented themselves.

She was well on her way to making a name for herself in Los Angeles. Above all, she was known for the stunning weddings that she orchestrated, and that was why Constance Bradford had been determined to work with her.

Alex was not a woman to whom money was a false god.

He sighed, then ran his hands through his hair. Like Phillip, Alex had defied her parents, and from what Sean had been able to find out, her relationship with both her mother and father had been strained for a good many years. Alex had simply proved her point, that she couldn't be controlled by her family or their money.

That she'd done it all on her own without her father's influence pleased him immensely.

Sean smiled slowly as he remembered talking with James Michaels at a party. The man would be a formidable opponent, so Alex wasn't lacking in courage.

Sean understood the need to prove yourself. If things had happened differently in his own family, he probably would have had to take time away from his own father, found his feet on his own. But things had been so different, there had never been time to do anything other than exactly what he had done....

He watched the sun climb higher into the sky and thought about ordering up a pot of coffee, then continued to stare out over the lightening skyline, his thoughts consumed with

Alexandra Michaels and what he was going to do about this whole mess.

Find Phillip. Far easier said than done. Phillip, aside from his fledgling advertising business, had worked in computers for many years. The money was excellent, and it had given him financial independence from his little tyrant of a father. Now, he had chosen to work one more job before the wedding, but there were strings attached.

The company that he worked for, Stealthco, was putting in a bid to design the software for the Stealth bomber. Phillip had flown to Virginia days after their talk. Now he was holed up at one of the company's private homes. No one would be let out until the bidding commenced. That way, it was impossible for information to be leaked, enabling other companies to modify their bids accordingly and capture the job.

Phillip had explained it all very carefully and told Sean that bidding commenced three days before the wedding started. In the meantime, he would be in a forced seclusion. In the beginning, the job had seemed a good thing. Even if Phillip had been tempted to see Muffy, he wouldn't have been able to.

Tell Muffy. Sean immediately rejected that idea. The girl was as nervous as an overbred poodle. Constance had really done quite a neat piece of psychological work on her daughter, turning her into a pale shadow of what she might have been. Muffy was high-strung in the extreme, and the thought of trying to talk her into letting just one other person in on the big secret behind her wedding filled Sean with a sick sense of dread. He couldn't do it to her.

Phillip and Muffy were counting on him. Their happiness was in his hands. And Constance Bradford was nothing if not a formidable opponent. She worked behind the scenes, lacking any real power except what she had through her husband. But she knew how to wield a certain type of power and was quite effective at what she did. Controlling people was something she was an expert at, and Muffy was her prize pawn.

He couldn't put Phillip and Muffy in jeopardy. Their future was too important. Even if the woman he wanted might be slipping through his fingers, Sean was nothing if not a loyal friend.

Alexandra. She was beautiful, but it wasn't only her beauty that had attracted him. Though *that* had hit him at first, right between the eyes. She had seemed so beautiful and vulnerable when he had first seen her in the office that day. She chose her words carefully when she spoke, with a self-protective hesitancy that had gone straight to his heart.

Her eyes. Intelligent and dark, hiding secrets. Hiding passion. She'd come alive in his arms, then frosted over into the coolly efficient Ms. Michaels, director of catering.

An enigma. An unmarried enigma. She didn't belong to any man—yet. Though he couldn't understand why. She had never married, and that was a puzzle to him, as well. He could discount her earlier years, as she had been climbing in her profession and had probably not given too much thought to her personal life. But in the last few years...

With his luck, the way things had been going, Mr. Wonderful would walk straight in the door before this whole fiasco was over, and she would fall madly in love with him.

And he, Sean, would never have another chance.

Sean unclenched his hands and took in a slow, steadying breath. The idea shook him to the core. He didn't want Alex to be with any man but himself. He wanted to place himself squarely between her and any other man.

Alex was not a woman a man dated casually. She was the kind of woman you looked at, then looked at again and quickly decided to spend the rest of your life with.

And he had to be that man.

Suddenly restless and eager for the day to begin, he walked over to the phone and punched out the numbers for room service. Then, after ordering coffee and a full breakfast, he hung up the phone and started for the shower.

The sooner he could get dressed and get out of his private suite, the sooner he could see Alex.

A plan was already beginning to form in his mind.

"So, EXACTLY HOW CLOSE are we supposed to get to our clients, Alex?"

Alex willed herself not to snap back with a sharp retort. Louise, a smugly self-satisfied grin on her face, was almost her undoing. But she was a master at concealing her emotions, and this little razor-sharp barb was certainly not going to be the exception to the rule.

"As close as you feel is necessary to get the job done." She smiled as she remembered one of her psychology professors. Jeff Downey had been endlessly entertaining, and she had emulated his style when she had begun to make presentations in front of large groups of people.

"How close is that?" Louise crooned.

Marcy, ever alert, glanced back at Louise with a hint of malice in her brilliant green eyes. "A lot closer than you've been getting to your clients, Louise. I don't think some of them even remember your name."

People coughed, feet shifted and someone let out a small snort of laughter before stifling it.

Louise's brittle blue eyes narrowed, then she directed her next attack at Alex. "Isn't there some kind of dress code for the *secretaries* around here, Alex? I mean, how are we supposed to command respect when she comes to work dressed like that?"

No one in the room had any doubts that she was speaking about Marcy. Marcy loved fashion and lived for sales.

Today, the woman in question was dressed as the perfect punkette, with a tight black skirt, a shaggy animal-print sweater in raw shades, footless black leggings and pointy-heeled, fifties-style shoes. A plated razor blade dangled from one ear, and her foundation makeup was very pale, with her eyes outlined in black kohl pencil and her lips a dark claret.

But on Marcy, the entire effect was stunning. She was a chameleon, just the other day having come in as a modified Gibson girl, with her bright red curls tamed into an up-sweep, and wearing a Laura Ashley pinafore.

And she was the only one in the entire office who thought the idea of a Renaissance wedding was great fun.

But Marcy was not to be ruffled. "It's *personal assistant* to you, Louise. And at least I don't come to work looking like I just blew in from the beach."

"Why, you little—"

"A sunscreen would really help, Louise. It would head off the rest of the damage—"

"Enough."

Both women stopped, Marcy turning around to face Alex, Louise sulkily staring out the window.

"Does anyone have any more questions about the Bradford wedding?" Alex glanced around the crowded conference room, then began to gather up her notes. "Just remember, it's to be given top priority for the next few weeks. This is a real honor, the Biltmore getting this particular job. I want you all to know I'm well aware of what all of you do to make me look good. And I won't forget any of it when it comes time to write up your personal reports."

There were a few contented murmurs, and Alex smiled as she looked out over the group of familiar faces.

"Short of painting cherubs on the ceiling, we'll make the people attending this wedding feel like they've stepped back in time. Now, let's get to work."

Alex had no illusions about the work she did or her particular abilities. She knew one of her talents was motivating people, and that was why she usually held monthly meetings more than once a month. She was considerate of her staff, and they responded by giving their all—with the exception of Louise.

Her little trick questions today had been ugly, and Alex began to seriously think about letting her go.

As she walked back to her office, Marcy fell into step beside her.

"Alex, do you have problems with the way I dress?"

"No."

"Is it something that will hold me back?"

"Not here. I can't tell you the number of times some Beverly Hills matron has asked me where you got your sweater or 'those darling earrings.' Just keep working as hard as you do and you'll do just fine."

"ALEX? YOUR MOTHER."

Alex leaned back in her chair, then picked up the phone and punched the button that would open up the particular line.

"Hi, Mother."

"Hello, darling. I know you're busy, but I was wondering if we could pencil in a dinner sometime this month."

"Let me get my calendar."

They chatted for a few minutes about inconsequential things, then Alex found a free day two weeks from Thursday, and she penciled it in.

"I thought the Bistro Garden. How does that sound to you, Alex?"

Alex thought of the bubbling fountain, the mountains of flowers and the bright patio umbrellas, then nodded her head. "I'd like that."

"I thought we could have a nice time, just the two of us." There was a slightly vulnerable, pleading note to her voice.

"All right. I'll see you there at eight."

"Thank you, darling."

After her mother hung up the phone, Alex stared at it for almost a minute. *I wonder why we're always harder on our mothers. I wonder if I will ever find it in my heart to for-give her.*

The dinner date would be a start. With a sigh, she picked up some of the papers on her desk and plunged back into business.

"LIGHTING UP another one? I thought you didn't smoke." The woman's soft voice was amused.

"I don't. Not usually, I mean. Just nervous, I guess." Phillip's long fingers shook slightly as he raised the ciga-rette to his lips.

"What's to be nervous about? We've got the deal. I'm sure our bid is the most reasonable."

Phillip sighed, then gazed out at the smoky, blue-gray rolling hills surrounding the farmhouse. Tucked away deep in the Virginia countryside, it had seemed the perfect place to isolate the members of the Stealthco team. Now, worried about how the wedding was going and how Muffy was holding up, Phillip wasn't sure he was going to be able to wait as patiently as he'd thought he could.

There was nothing wrong with telling Rachel. She was a close friend as well as a co-worker, and she would never be-tray a confidence.

Quickly, he outlined the entire plan to her, as well as a little of how he was feeling.

Rachel was impressed.

"This is one of the most romantic things I've ever heard. I mean, half my girlfriends can't even get the men in their lives to talk about marriage, and the other half can't get their husbands detached from their recliners. And you're doing all this just to protect Muffy from her mother?"

Phillip took one last draw from the cigarette, then ground it out in the ashtray by his side. One thing about these forced isolations, there was no comfort that wasn't anticipated and provided for.

"She's a pretty nasty piece of work. I tried the formal route. Her father was pleased with me. He's a mild sort of man, and I think he genuinely does want Muffy to be happy. But the minute Constance heard that I wasn't going into my father's business, she sabotaged the whole thing."

"And Muffy wouldn't just run away with you? It'd be a lot simpler."

"She's an only child. I don't think Constance particularly enjoyed being a mother. She's a very controlling woman, and Muffy has been under her thumb from the time she was born. It's not that she's weak—there's something more than that going on. Constance controls her, makes all the decisions, manipulates her."

"And Muffy allows that to happen."

"It's not as easy as all that, Rachel. That mother of hers..." He stared out at the mountains, then spoke very softly, fighting to keep the emotion out of his voice.

"You know, there were times when I suspected her mother was abusing her. Physically. I asked Muffy, but she begged me not to talk about it, and I couldn't bear to see her so upset. It scares me, sometimes, to think about this whole crazy idea not working, about Constance finding out and punishing her...."

"There will come a time," Rachel said quietly, "when Muffy will have to stand up to her mother herself, you know."

"I know. But I get scared."

"Of course you do."

"She's got to get away from her influence first."

Rachel nodded. A cool brunette, she had a quiet, self-assured strength that could be counted on in times of crisis. When things got crazy during the course of developing a new project, Phillip had always admired the way this woman managed to keep her head and think clearly. It was a quality he didn't always possess, particularly if he was emotionally involved.

Rachel, as always, said the practical thing. "Look, it's almost time for dinner. You'll feel better with a full stomach. There's really nothing you can do for now. I'm sure your friend has everything under control."

"ALEX? IT'S COLLEEN." Marcy's voice was brisk.

Alex felt the smile forming on her lips as she picked up the phone, happiness bubbling up inside her, filling her up. Colleen Michaels, her aunt and godmother, was her favorite person in the world.

"Colleen! You're back!"

Her aunt travelled all over the world with her uncle Charles. Unable to have children of their own, the two of them had played a major part in Alex's childhood. Although her uncle still ran a flight school at one of Los Angeles's major airports, he had given over the supervision of the school to his partner. Now he and Colleen had the opportunity to see the world.

Colleen breezed in and out of Alex's life, and Alex adored her. Even when Alex had been a child, her aunt had encouraged her to think for herself and do what she thought was right. These qualities had not always endeared her to Alex's mother and father.

"Just for a week, then it's off to Venice. I think Charlie is going to invest in a film. But we'll only be gone about ten days."

"Does my father know?"

"Not yet. But I'm sure he will."

Alex threw back her head and laughed, delighted at the image of her father's face when he discovered that his "crazy brother Charlie" was up to another of his schemes. But they were good schemes, designed to help him and everyone around him live life to the fullest and enjoy every minute.

"Can you get away for dinner?" Colleen came straight to the point. If anything characterized her life and Charlie's, it was that they lived it as if determined not to waste a minute. And they had the money to do it in style.

"Yes." Alex made up her mind instantly. She liked to see her aunt whenever she had the chance, and she was cowardly enough that she didn't want to see Sean. She knew he'd probably come down to her office shortly, and she didn't want to have to talk him out of having dinner with her. Dinner with Colleen, and perhaps a talk, would help put things in perspective.

"When?"

"Sevenish."

"Where?"

"Chin Chins."

"Are we taking Beluga?"

"I couldn't leave him at home. You know how he loves those dumplings."

"I'll see you there."

"SHE'S NOT HERE, Mr. Lawton. She left for a dinner date."

Sean felt his insides tightening as he looked down at the woman with the razor blade hanging from her ear. It had taken him only two visits to the catering offices to realize that this woman, who had a wardrobe that rivaled the late Liberace's, was probably the person closest to Alex.

He had to know, but at the same time hated exposing his vulnerability. "Do you . . . know who she went out with?"

He watched the darkly glossed, claret-colored lips break into a genuine smile. She was on to him—but she wasn't going to use it against him.

Perhaps he'd found an ally.

"Her aunt, Colleen Michaels. She just got back from Africa with Alex's Uncle Charlie."

"The Charlie Michaels that runs that flight school?"

"One and the same."

He was about to ask where they had planned to have dinner when Marcy said softly, "Alex really treasures her time with her aunt. She hasn't seen her in a couple of months."

That decided him. He would wait until tomorrow. But then . . .

"I'd like to schedule an appointment with Alex tomorrow. To talk about the first of those three parties."

Marcy smiled up at him. He knew, from the look in her green eyes, that she didn't believe a word of it, but was enjoying herself immensely.

"What time?"

"I'd like to be her latest appointment."

"That would be six. It's taken."

He took a breath, but before he could speak, Marcy, her pencil skimming swiftly down the columns in the large appointment book, said softly, "But I could call Mrs. Kinkaid and ask her if she could come in at four, instead. I think I can persuade her, tell her something else has come up. Why don't I buzz you tomorrow morning and let you know?"

"That would be perfect. I appreciate it, Marcy."

"I know you do." The green eyes were bright with mischief. "And if I thought I had a chance with a guy like you, I'd jump at it. But as long as you want Alex . . ." She gave a shrug that he found so vulnerably appealing that he put his hand on her shoulder, very gently.

"I do have a little brother, and he'll be here for the wedding. I'm sure I could manage to introduce you to each other."

"Does he look like you?"

"Better. He's younger. Not as burned out."

Marcy's eyes sparkled. "Okay. What's his name?"

"Brian."

"Does he have eyes like yours?"

"Exactly."

Marcy sighed. "And who says good deeds go unrewarded?"

THE PARKING LOT behind Chin Chins on Sunset was packed, but Colleen managed to find a place to park her Mercedes. She had called ahead and ordered the food, and Alex went inside to pick it up, then brought it back to the car.

They could have eaten inside, except for one rather large problem.

Beluga. An enormous black Chow Chow, Colleen had bought him at a pet store on impulse. She'd told Charlie that the fluffy puppy had "looked so lonely and unhappy in that glass cage I just had to let him out." It had made perfect sense to Charlie, and Beluga had become a member of their family.

Unfortunately, Beluga was bad news at Chin Chins. Colleen had been able to persuade the waiters that Beluga, as huge and fluffy and intimidating as he was, should be able to sit with her at the outside tables that lined the sidewalk. But Beluga, a totally ungrateful reprobate when it came to matters of the stomach, had waited until Colleen was deep in conversation with a friend before snatching a chicken-and-onion dumpling with cilantro sauce off a neighboring table.

When the man in question had complained, Beluga had growled, and his fate had been sealed.

Thus, at Chin Chins, they ate in the car. Which was fine with Beluga, if uncomfortable for Colleen and Alex.

"So I hear you're handling the Bradford wedding," Colleen said as Alex settled the white cartons of Chinese food between them.

"Did Mother tell you?"

"She's proud of you, Alex— Beluga, settle *down!* My God, let him get a whiff of that cilantro sauce and he goes wild."

Beluga, in the back seat, was performing his heartrending version of a starving dog.

"What a total ham," Alex said fondly, reaching back to scratch the dog behind his ears. Beluga swiped at her hand, his black tongue warm.

"You have to wait, Beluga, or you'll burn your mouth." Colleen turned her attention back to her niece. "The concept of nibbling at food is totally foreign to him."

"You look marvelous." And Alex meant it. Colleen was a complete contrast to both Alex and her mother. A delicate blonde, Colleen still had the perfectly sculpted, razor-cheeked fineness that made a person look twice. But she wasn't a pale blonde, à la Muffy Bradford. Her deep blue eyes were alive, dominating a face that Charlie Michaels said had captivated him from the moment he'd seen her.

"You do, too. Something's different. You look more... alive. On edge. Does that make sense?"

Alex could feel the beginnings of a smile. "It does."

"There's a man in your life." Colleen stated the fact as she began to open the bags containing an assortment of dumplings. Beluga put one massive paw on the back of the front seat and gave a piteous whine.

"How do you always know?"

"Alex, since you were a child you always had the most revealing face. Do you love him?" So like Colleen, to get straight to the point.

"I... I'm in lust with him."

Colleen dipped a chicken-and-onion dumpling into the cilantro sauce and carefully hand-fed it to Beluga. "I don't think I ever told you this, but the first time Charlie looked at me, I went weak at the knees. Lust. I wanted him. He made everything look sharper, brighter." Her blue eyes were suddenly soft, remembering. "He took my breath away, he was such a handsome man, so interested in everything life had to offer. Charlie was just so much fun to be around. He took me out for dinner that same night after the party, dinner turned into breakfast, and we were never apart after that."

"But you had a long engagement."

"Pooh. That was for your grandparents' sake. Charlie and I had everything figured out. I just knew that I didn't want to live in a world that didn't have Charlie Michaels in it. Yes, Beluga, you may have a won ton."

Alex slowly reached into the bag and drew out one of the dumplings, a combination of pork and shrimp. "But what about all the other stuff? Shared interests, similar backgrounds—"

"Charlie and I had plenty of shared interests. I was interested in him, and he was interested in me." She smiled, then reached over and grasped her niece's free hand. "*You* have been talking to your mother."

"We're going out to dinner in about two weeks."

"I have nothing against Meredith. She gave me much more time with you than either of us deserved. But she has one major flaw. You cannot constantly be careful. It doesn't work that way."

"Colleen, if I go after this man I may get hurt."

"Why? Does he have a wife stashed away in another state?"

"No. Not yet."

"Is there another woman?"

"Yes."

"When you look at them together, do they feel right?"

"I've never seen them together, but I don't think they feel right."

"Then what's holding you up? I'm sorry, Alex, if I sound cruel, but you cannot possibly live a careful life and not expect to die absolutely full of regrets."

"She's such a fragile thing. I don't know, I feel sorry for her."

"Very noble of you."

"It's not that easy."

"Isn't it? Alex, you look wonderful. Friskier. Healthier. I knew right away something had changed in your life. There's a gleam in your eye, and unless there's been a total change in your life-style you haven't told me about, that something *had* to be a man. And men like that don't come along every day. I don't want to see you throw away a chance on what I believe is the greatest happiness there is. There's *nothing* more exciting than having the right man in your life."

"I know, I know." Alex looked down, miserable. She had shredded two paper napkins and was starting on a third. Her dumpling felt like a lump of thick dough in the pit of her stomach. "I wish I could be more daring, but I get so damn scared—"

"We all do. Oh, Alex, do you think I wasn't the most scared little thing in the world when I walked into that party and saw Charlie? He *overwhelmed* me! There were times when I wanted to get away from him as desperately as I wanted to be close to him. I can't tell you some of the fights we had—I felt like I was going to be consumed! It *is* scary, but I don't know of a better way to live life. A lot of what I am—the *best* of what I am—I owe to Charlie."

"So where do I start?"

"I think you might start by recognizing that you have something very special with this man. If nothing else, he makes you light up and look wonderful. Then I think you might consider spending some time with him, to see if he's as special as I think he's going to be."

"I'm just afraid of being overwhelmed—"

"Every woman should be overwhelmed some time in her life. Oh, Alex, I'm not saying you should stay with a man if he chooses to abuse you or treat you cruelly. I'm just saying that it looks like you have the start of something truly wonderful, and I'd hate to be talking with you a few years from now and listening to you say, 'if only'..."

Alex bit her lip and looked out the window. The parking lot afforded them a spectacular view of Los Angeles, lights twinkling in all directions. She could see the Beverly Center, could make out the shape of the Pacific Design Center, affectionately known as the Blue Whale.

She loved this city, and she loved her life, loved the hotel industry, especially catering. It was exciting, becoming intimately linked with different families for a short time, taking part in some of their happiest moments, whether they were weddings, bar mitzvahs, anniversaries.

But now she was so acutely aware that something was missing.

The feeling had started right before Sean had walked into her life.

Talk about being ready.

Now, she either had to do something about it or watch him walk out of her life and regret . . .

No.

In comparison with possible regrets, being hurt seemed a small price to pay.

"I'll try."

"Oh, Alex, don't let me push you around. I just want you to be happy. That's all."

"I know."

"Another dumpling?"

"No, thanks."

"That's a good sign. I couldn't eat when I met Charlie. That first dinner, and then that breakfast, all I did was push food around on my plate."

Alex sighed. "Give my dumplings to Beluga."

"I'll take some of them home to Charlie."

After kissing her aunt goodbye and giving Beluga one last pat, Alex walked slowly to her car. She waved as Colleen pulled out of the parking lot, then unlocked the driver's side of her silver Mercedes and slid inside.

Guiltily, as if she expected her aunt to drive back into the parking lot, Alex reached beneath the seat and pulled out the book she had bought at Crown, wrapped in its bland plastic bag.

There has to be a way to understand all of this. There has to be a logic to it.

She eased the book out of the bag and studied it. The cover design was bold, with large curling print. There was a picture below the title, of a man and a woman embracing. The blurb across the front proclaimed: "At last! The book that explains what really goes on between men and women and how they can break free of restricting patterns and attain real intimacy!"

She had a pile of these books by her bed, slid beneath it when she suspected anyone might be coming over. Even Karin didn't know about this secret reading habit. Books like *Smart Women, Foolish Choices* and *Men Who Hate Women and the Women Who Love Them.*

Most nights, when she had a little time to read, she would pull one of them out. Or, if the thought of pondering the whole man-woman thing was too depressing, she would pick up one of the cookbooks she regularly borrowed from Karin and read that.

She wondered what Colleen would think of her trying to get answers out of a book. But Alex wanted to be sure. She didn't want to make a mistake. Again, she wanted to know the rules.

As a young child, she had spent a great deal of time with Charlie and Colleen. Her father had traveled and had wanted her mother along. A child would have been an inconvenience. Thank God for Colleen, who had been delighted to take the little girl into her home.

Then later, Alex had been regularly sent away to camp, then boarding school. She didn't have a whole lot of experience watching men and women interact, except for her aunt and uncle. And even at an extremely young age, she had known that what Charlie and Colleen had was special.

Alex stared out the window for a few minutes, lost in thought, before she slid the book back inside the plastic bag and started up the car.

Maybe dinner. Just once.

Chapter Four

How could one man turn her life upside down, make her change her mind fifteen times in a single afternoon, infuriate her and endear himself to her all at the same time? It was beyond Alex's comprehension.

The books she secretly read late at night had never come up against a man like Sean Lawton.

But the new, brave, self-assured Alex, who was going to live her life with no regrets—hadn't Marcy had a pair of jeans by that name?—was going to be in charge of her life. In control. Poised, calm and assured.

"Have dinner with me tonight, Alex," Sean had said.

"No, I don't think so," she had replied uncertainly.

"That was really good, Alex," she said to herself as she drove along the 10 Freeway West toward Santa Monica. In order to punish herself for being such a total dip about Sean's dinner invitation, she'd decided to go to a party Karin and Jesse had told her about. In Malibu.

It would be in one of those houses overlooking the ocean, she could check out who was catering the party, see if their food was as good as what the Biltmore offered, and maybe, just maybe, there would be a man who would be magnificent enough to make her forget all about Sean.

"AND AFTER EIGHT YEARS of therapy, Alex, I think I'm finally ready to face the world again."

The face was boyish, deeply tanned, with the beginnings of slight jowls around the jaw. The hairline was receding, the body soft and pudgy, and the blue eyes faded, the expression in them slightly bored. *This* was a man to make her forget Sean? This guy could make her forget she had any desire to communicate with the rest of the human race.

Spotting Karin, she waved a slightly desperate hello, then turned to Mr. Therapy.

"Gee, Howard, I hate to leave, but a friend of mind just came in and I'd better go say hello."

Howard nodded amiably, an emotional vampire already on the lookout for his next victim.

Once Alex connected with Karin and Jesse, she didn't leave their sides.

"Alex, parties mean mingling. Why aren't you out getting to know some of the men?" Karin chided her gently.

"I'm fine. Did you try this salmon pâté? I wonder where they got it."

"Don't change the subject. Look at that guy over there. He's kind of cute. Alex, he's looking at you."

"Okay, okay. I'll wander that way."

Later, she wondered why she had even decided to attend this party. It was as if someone had rounded up all the strange men in the city and led them straight to her.

"Then, when my mother's second husband decided to take me on, I realized that my inherent masculinity was too much for him."

"What are you? Cancer? Scorpio? You have water-sign eyes, do you know that?"

"So, are you going home with anybody after this thing is over?"

That last line had done her in. She had raced for the door and out to her car, then broken all speed records to get home. After feeding Roscoe and taking a long hot shower, she jumped into bed with a cookbook. Nothing about men and women tonight. She might make a pile of every self-help book she possessed and start a bonfire.

No, tonight she was going to immerse herself in the wonderful world of Scandinavian baking. Alex read recipes voraciously, wondering which ones she could talk Pierre into experimenting with. Visions of Danish Apple Cake, Strawberry Cones, Swedish Chocolate Frosted Almond Bars and Meringue Tortes danced through her head as she furiously read, then, tired beyond belief, she set the book down and turned off the light.

But she couldn't sleep.

"Stop biting my toes," she mumbled to Roscoe. Whenever she tossed and turned, he had the annoying habit of chewing on her feet. Once in a while he would use his claws, but that was only if he really thought she was disturbing his beauty sleep.

What is going to happen to me? She rolled over in bed and stared at the ceiling. The men at the party could have been from Central Casting. The new, improved psychotic-delusional type, along with your standard nerd thrown in for good measure. And no Los Angeles party would be complete without your classic New Age Sensitive Male Animal.

"Water-sign eyes, what a bunch of bull," she muttered again, punching her pillow.

It was frightening to her how her aunt's philosophy was beginning to make sense. There weren't that many men out in the world who were both truly spectacular and also *did* something for her. What could happen if she simply went out with Sean? After all, they would be in a public place. It wasn't as if he was going to try and jump her bones in a restaurant.

But after fourteen—no, make that almost fifteen months of celibacy—even that didn't look too bad.

"I give up," she said softly to the empty room, not even waking the snoring Roscoe. "I tried. I really did. And it's not as if I'll be taking him away from Muffy."

She closed her eyes and, exhausted, finally slept.

SHE WAITED FOR SEAN to come to her office the entire day, but at six-fifteen when he didn't show, Alex finally had to admit to herself she just might have blown it.

"Anything else, Alex?" Marcy said over the intercom.

"Just bring me in the menu for the Bradford wedding. I want to look it over one more time."

When Marcy entered the office, she had already changed. This morning, it had been pure classics all the way. The red curls had been tamed into an approximation of a Grace Kelly chignon. The shirt had been silk, the sweater cashmere, the slacks wool flannel. Small gold earrings and understated makeup had completed the look, along with Italian leather shoes.

But now, having changed to go out with Peter, Marcy was dressed in what Alex teasingly referred to as her Cat Woman outfit. Black leggings and a skinny rib black tank top, topped with a fingertip-length fake leopard-skin coat. High, high, ankle strap, leopard-print pumps, huge gold hoops and tawny makeup.

Looking at her assistant as she watched her glide into her office, Alex wondered if Marcy ever had the same problems with men as she did.

"Marcy," she said carefully as she took the sheaf of papers from her. "What do you do if you're at a party and you get stuck with a real jerk and you can't seem to get rid of him?"

One shoulder lifted in an extremely expressive shrug. "I tell him to buzz off. Get lost. It's all in your attitude, Alex."

Some things couldn't be faked. A few minutes after Marcy left, Alex sighed and sat back in her chair. Then, knowing she was totally alone on the floor, she gave in to the impulse, unpinned her hair, kicked off her heels and swung her aching feet up on her desk.

SEAN WALKED SILENTLY down the corridor, his footsteps muffled by the thick carpet. He carried a large shopping bag in his arms, and he started to grin as he rounded the corner and saw the light coming from beneath Alex's door.

This time she couldn't turn him down without seeming unspeakably rude. And one thing he sensed very strongly about Alexandra Michaels, she was never rude if she could help it.

The door was partially open when he reached it, and he peeked inside.

His heart melted.

Alex was sitting in her chair, her feet up, fast asleep.

He entered the room slowly, then set the shopping bag down just inside the door and walked quietly over to her desk. The lamplight illuminated her face, and Sean could see the lines of exhaustion, the tightness around her mouth even in sleep. There was something so heartbreakingly vulnerable about her when she didn't know she was being watched.

He was surprised by the rush of feeling just looking at her engendered. He wanted to take care of her, and all he had done so far was to cause her grief. There were plenty of other women who wouldn't have cared that he was engaged, would have gone ahead and been delighted to have an affair. Some wouldn't have even cared once he was married. He'd run with a fast, cynical set for far too long.

The last thing he had ever wanted to become was a cynic. But he had.

Strangely enough, he'd always believed that fate sent you exactly what you needed, when you needed it.

He'd despaired of ever finding a woman he could fall in love with. He'd agreed to this charade of a wedding because he was the perfect stand-in for Phillip—incapable of deep feeling for a woman.

Then the gods had sent him Alexandra. How they must be laughing at him now. The intense, totally emotional feelings that were flooding his heart made him feel like he was all of sixteen years old, his heart in his mouth as he asked for a dance.

He studied her face for several minutes, then remembering he had hot food in the bag, he set to work creating dinner for her.

Not wanting to wake her, Sean looked around her office. There was a small table just outside the door that would be perfect. Then, if he was careful not to make too much noise when he opened her office door wider...

SHE WAS DREAMING, dreaming she had died and gone to heaven. Heaven was like one long, continuous party, only all the food was good and the men were interesting to talk to.

But the food! The smells were...

Cautiously, in that strange state between sleeping and waking, Alex slowly opened one eye.

Sean was lighting two candles on a small, round table covered with a peach-colored cloth. A cloth that looked suspiciously like one of the tablecloths in Pierre's restaurant.

She moved in the chair, and it creaked. Sean looked back over his shoulder, and their eyes met.

What was he doing here? Alex slowly lowered her legs off the desk. She tried to stuff her feet back into her pumps, but they were slightly swollen and so she left them bare.

She glanced back up at him, and her confusion must have been in her eyes because Sean broke the silence.

"You wouldn't go out to dinner with me, so I decided to bring dinner to you."

Something about his utter persistence was immensely gratifying. She got up from behind her desk and walked toward the small, intimate setting.

He smiled, then pulled her chair out for her. She sat down, grateful that he kept his hands to himself, didn't try to accidentally touch her. Her nap had refreshed her, and she felt strangely competent to deal with whatever he threw her way.

She just wanted to spend a little more time with him. See what was beneath that beautiful masculine exterior. Talk to him. Somewhere along the line Sean would slip up, and she would consign him to the ranks of Mr. Therapy or Mr. Astrology. Then it would be easy to forget him.

You wish.

"That's not food I'm familiar with," she said softly. "Do you cook?"

"I didn't cook this," he said, answering her question. "It's from the Seventh Street Bistro."

"Oh." He was really clever, and she was impressed. She knew the restaurant; Pierre knew the chef. Sleek and high-ceilinged, the restaurant also had changing exhibits of modern art as well as quite artistic cuisine. She had eaten there once with her godmother—they had not let Beluga in—and had remembered the food as exquisite.

"Their chef trained at Maxim's," Sean said as he began to open one of the beautifully boxed meals.

Alex was well aware that the Bistro had a reputation for the classiest takeout in town.

"I wasn't sure what you liked, so I ordered a little of everything. Potato pancakes with Sevruga caviar and lemon cream, salmon tartar with ginger and green peppercorns—"

"I like that all so far—"

"Cold poached salmon with herb dressing and goat cheese, mahimahi with spices, broccoli ravioli in a butter-lobster sauce—"

"Oh, my God—"

"And last but not least, venison with a peach-and-apple chutney in a black peppercorn sauce. Is there anything you don't like?"

She started to laugh. "No. I can be a real pig."

"I like a girl with a healthy appetite."

She laughed then, knowing that this was simply gentle teasing, that there wasn't any hidden sexual innuendo or sleazy message she had to figure out. Then there was silence as they both did justice to the food. Sean had brought china plates, silverware, linen napkins, two tall white candles in silver candlesticks and a centerpiece of tiger lilies.

Alex couldn't remember enjoying a dinner more.

He kept her wineglass filled, but when she finally put her hand over it as he raised the bottle, he didn't force any more on her.

"Why a catering career?" he asked, once they had both eaten to take the edge off their hunger.

"Why not?" She laughed, then reached for her wineglass. "I was working at a bookstore and making minimum wage. A friend of mine was making terrific money as a cocktail waitress down at the Marriott. She told me there was an opening, so I took it. Then I figured out that the bartender made even more money, and I began to watch the way she made all the drinks. She gave two weeks' notice, and I asked her to give me some on-the-job training.

"After I convinced my boss that I could bartend, I did so for a year and a half, then moved on to another hotel. That was when I began to take an interest in catering. By the time I took a job here, I was one step away from the director of catering. Five years later, I had the job."

She took another sip of wine, then said, "So now you have to tell me."

"About what?"

"Why construction? Why buying and selling city buildings? What is it that caught you?"

"I like making deals." He leaned back in his chair, studying her. "Sometimes it isn't even the building, though I like to take them and make them over into what I want them to be. It's the challenge of getting something of quality and turning it into something even better."

"Pretty ruthless."

"I can be—when I want something badly enough."

"This ravioli is incredible."

"You're very good at changing the subject, Alex. But I want you to know something. Making you uncomfortable was never my intention. I just want to get to know you. I wish circumstances could have been different, I wish we could have met at a different time. We didn't, but I still want to know you. I'm not going to hurt you. I give you my word."

"I wish we'd met at a different time, too," she whispered. "You're not like any man I've ever met."

That seemed to please him. "I want you to know, Alex, that you're totally in control here. Nothing is going to happen if you don't want it to. I'm not here for any ulterior motive other than getting to know you."

"Really?" She was astonished by his honesty. "You haven't thought about—"

"Well, I have, but I'd have to be dead if I hadn't thought about that."

"What does marriage mean to you, Sean?" she asked quietly.

"Forever. Loyalty and courage. Steadfastness. Standing by that person's side and facing life together. Wanting to be with that person more than anyone else in the world."

"Muffy's a lucky girl."

He had the funniest look on his face. She couldn't quite define it.

"Yes, she is," he said quietly. Then, he seemed to check himself, as if he didn't want to say any more.

"I get the feeling that she's a little cowed by her mother. Sometimes, when they're both in here for consultations, I feel so sorry for her."

"I think she needs to get away from Constance. The woman is venomous. I wonder how Muffy has survived."

"I know. I still can't quite get a handle on her."

They ate in silence for a while before conversation resumed.

"Do you think," Alex began carefully, "that it's possible for a man and a woman to be good friends?"

"No."

"That's kind of sexist."

"It's the truth."

"Could we be—"

"The way I feel about you, no."

"Then why are we having dinner together? Is this some kind of experiment? A game?" She could feel herself getting upset.

He glanced away from her, and frustration was evident in every muscle in his face, the way he held his body, the sense of coiled-up energy.

"God, Alex, if I told you the truth, *I* wouldn't even believe it."

"Try me."

"I can't."

"Are you in love with her?" The words were out of her mouth before she had time to check them, but she had to know.

He was silent for a moment, and his tone was subdued when he answered her.

"No."

She could almost feel what that admission had cost him, emotionally. "Yet you're going to marry her. Does Muffy know this?"

"No—and you're not going to tell her anything or let her know that we talked about her wedding. It would only upset her."

"Don't you think it's going to upset her when she finds out you married her and don't love her?"

"I *do* love her. As a friend. But not the way I—not the way a man loves the woman he commits himself to."

"Do you love anyone but yourself?" Now she was getting angry, and she knew these were fighting words.

"You wouldn't believe me if I told you."

The meaning of his words took a minute to sink in, and then she was staring at him, her heart speeding up as she finally understood.

"Me?"

He nodded.

"You love me?"

"It's different for a man."

"I guess so!"

"I don't know how to explain it myself. I just looked at you and I knew. And I don't believe in wasting time."

How like Colleen, she thought suddenly, then grinned. Colleen and Charlie would love this man.

"Why the smile?"

"You remind me of the two people I love most in the world."

"Your father and mother?"

"My aunt and uncle."

"Charlie and Colleen, right?"

"How did you know? Oh, that's right. You had me investigated."

"Forgive me that, Alex. I had my reasons."

"I'm sure you did."

"Are you going to stay for dessert?"

"And more of this conversation? I wouldn't miss it, it beats water-sign eyes all to hell."

"I beg your pardon?"

"Private joke."

Dessert consisted of two pieces of Pierre's incredible chocolate torte. Alex recognized one of his waiters after he thoughtfully knocked and walked in, then cleared away their dishes and placed the two dessert dishes on the peach table-cloth.

After he had left them alone, Alex leaned back in her chair and picked up her wineglass, swirling what was left of her wine.

"The tablecloth, the flowers, the silver, the china—it's from Pierre, isn't it?"

"A very accommodating man, your Pierre."

"A traitor."

"He understands that sometimes our hearts take us places and we have no choice but to follow."

That totally silenced her. She set her wineglass down and sat forward. "I'm really trying to understand this, Sean. I really am. What do you want from me?"

"Just this." As he leaned forward, all power and intensity, Alex realized she must be getting a taste of the way he did business.

He's making another deal. Only it's not a building, it's me.

"All I want from you," he said slowly, "is a promise that you'll see me until the wedding and not go out with any other man."

Dead silence reigned until Alex delicately cleared her throat.

"What's in it for me?"

"The beginning of the best time both of us will ever have."

She smiled. He had guts, she had to hand that to him. "Can I give you some conditions?"

"We'll see."

"No sex. I'm deadly serious about that one, Sean."

"I agree. Anything else?"

"I don't want to hurt Muffy."

"I'm in total agreement with you there."

"So," she said as she picked up her fork and cut into the rich layers of her dessert, "you've been honest with me, so I'll be honest with you."

"I'd appreciate it."

"I am totally out of my depth with you. Do you make these kinds of arrangements with all the women you go out with?"

"No." His gaze was unwavering. "Most of the women I've been with couldn't have cared whether I was engaged, married or single. It wasn't a major consideration as long as they thought they had access to my money."

"I see. I must strike you as tremendously gauche."

"Not at all. You're quite a refreshing change."

"So then what we have is a friendship, right? A male-female relationship without sex."

"No. It's not friendship, Alex. I'm just asking you not to go out and do something foolish with any other man before the wedding."

"*This* strikes me as kind of foolish. But why does it feel so right?"

"Will you trust me on this one, Alex? It would mean . . . everything to me."

You, Alex, are certifiably insane to agree to this little arrangement.

Thus, Alexandra Michaels—who needed a soccer rule book when she went away to camp, who carefully wrote out lists with her perfect handwriting and left them scattered all over her otherwise immaculate office and home, who didn't like to dive into a deep pool without first checking whether there were rocks or not, who had only learned to overcome her natural hesitancy to trying new foods when Pierre insisted she was the only person on the staff who understood what he was trying to do in his kitchen—Alex of the long lists, the perfectly ordered home and the stacks of self-help books beneath her bed—found herself agreeing to do as Sean said.

And she couldn't even blame the wine.

YOU, SEAN, are certifiably insane to agree to this little arrangement. No sex? What are you, crazy?

Now that he had agreed to keep their relationship platonic, Sean found he couldn't think of anything else. Yet he knew that he couldn't take advantage of Alex that way, not when she thought he was going to marry Muffy.

He didn't want her to think of him as a total bastard, but none of it seemed to matter when he saw himself doomed to over two months of waiting.

They were adults. What he wanted to do, if he was perfectly honest with himself, was to spirit her away and make her his in the most basic way there was. His dreams were tortuous. They were simple dreams, with two people starring in them, over and over again. Graphic dreams. Explicit dreams. He woke up every morning and wondered how he could have agreed to such a thing.

He was a walking testosterone bomb, and he knew it.

And Phillip was still in seclusion. Why couldn't his friend have taken on a less complicated job, like doubling for Arnold Schwarzenegger? Why did Phillip have to be in hiding somewhere on the East Coast, unable to come to the phone?

Sean contemplated every possibility. Carrier pigeons. Talking drums—they always worked in the jungle movies, didn't they? Even smoke signals. But there was no way he could reach Phillip.

He was consigned to a hell of his own making.

Sean Lawton, media darling, could buy and sell almost any building he chose in Los Angeles. He'd faced some of the most powerful men in the city over the bargaining tables, and he had almost always won.

How strange that one woman was going to bring him to his knees.

SHE WAS STUDYING the proposed flower order for the Bradford wedding—all one hundred and twenty-five thousand dollars' worth—when a slice of her favorite lemon cake was set down in front of her nose.

Alex remained silent as long as she could, but finally couldn't stand it any longer.

"Traitor."

"You Americans get so worked up over so many little things."

"Like marriage?"

"He's not at the altar yet, *chérie.*"

"Pierre, you think like a typical man. All you guys are the same."

"I will tell you something, Alex." Now Pierre was perched on her desk, so Alex had no choice but to put down the order and contemplate the piece of cake. It was giving off the most tantalizing lemon fragrance. Pierre was a master of manipulation. He knew that she had been pining for a piece of this cake. It was one he usually only made in the spring and summer.

Alex knew she was lost. She picked up the fork. No use letting a perfectly good piece of cake go to waste.

"There aren't any aphrodisiacs in this thing, are there?"

"*Chérie,* you wound me! But I am going to tell you something—"

"And it is for my own good."

"How did you know?" He looked genuinely puzzled.

"You *always* tell me it's for my own good."

"Well, it is. Here is what I, Pierre, think. I have thought about the two of you, especially while I have been making my desserts. It doesn't match. Sean and that Muffy. He is like a rich, dark piece of chocolate cake, while she is like a white cake with no taste. A *dry* white cake."

Alex winced. That was Pierre's ultimate insult.

"You, Alex, are a lighter chocolate, perhaps even a spice cake. But there is life to you, there is body and richness. You are like a delicate piece of cake, but one is surprised when one bites into it, for there is more flavor than one suspected at first.''

''Yeah, and I have whipped cream for brains.''

''What happened? Did everything go smoothly the other night?''

''You might say that.''

''But not smoothly enough, eh? for you are still in a foul mood.''

''That is a decidedly sexist remark, Pierre.''

''Eat the lemon cake, Alex.''

''EAT THE LEMON CAKE, Alex,'' she mimicked, later on in bed, this time with an Asian cookbook. But Alex couldn't keep her mind on *Nori-Maki*, Tofu *Dengaku*, *Guchal Pan* or *Ngau Yuk Mai*.

''That about sums this whole mess up, Roscoe. *Ngau Yuk Mai*.''

Roscoe, who was about as empathetic as a brick wall, snored softly among the folds of the quilted bedspread.

''I really hate you,'' Alex said, glaring at the tabby cat.

In answer, Roscoe twitched his tail.

''Why can't you be a loving cat, like Morris in all those television commercials?''

More soft snores.

''Remember that story about the house that was burning down and that cat that woke the entire family up and none of them were killed in the fire because of that cat's bravery?''

More snores.

Alex snapped the cookbook shut, then turned off her bedside lamp. She burrowed down beneath the covers, and when Roscoe started to bite her toes, she kicked him.

''Go to sleep, you fleabag. And if the house catches on fire, it's every man for himself.''

Chapter Five

"Sean, this arrangement could be professional suicide for me." Alex kept her voice low as she spoke on the phone. She'd thought a great deal about what Sean had proposed. She also knew Pierre wouldn't have sent up just anyone to clear the private dinner table and deliver their dessert. She could trust Pierre to be discreet.

"I'm not asking you to do anything that will compromise you in anyone's eyes. I'm simply asking you to spend some extra time with me before the wedding and not see anyone else. No one will talk."

"But . . . Sean, that first night, when Louise walked into my office. I'm worried about what she might do."

"Has she done anything to you before?"

"No. But I've called her on neglecting some of the finer points of two weddings and an anniversary party. She was pretty nasty about it."

"How is her work performance now?"

"Substandard. To be perfectly honest, I've been thinking about firing her."

He was silent for a moment, then said, "I blocked her view of you. I don't think she saw anything. If you'd like, I'll think of a way to fix it."

"I'd appreciate it."

"Point her out to me when I'm in your office this afternoon, and I'll take a look at her. Sometimes a second opinion helps."

Her day went swiftly, and Alex knew she was buoyed up by the knowledge that Sean loved her. She still didn't understand how or why—even though some of the books she had read said that men fell in love on a purely emotional basis while women tended to look at the more practical sides of a relationship.

As it turned out, she didn't have to point Louise out to Sean after all. She came into Alex's office while Sean was there.

They were going over the fine points of Sean's first party, a bachelor affair, when Louise came in the door.

"Well, well, well, Alex, working another late night again?" Her tone was deliberately suggestive.

She obviously hadn't seen Sean. His back was to her, and he was hidden in the depths of one of the large, buttery-soft chairs in front of Alex's desk.

"Who are you?" he asked quietly, turning around and fixing his gaze on Louise.

She was startled, first by the realization that Sean was in Alex's office, then by his tone of voice. Louise opened her mouth to speak, but nothing came out.

"This is Louise Hartson. She's one of the assistant catering managers."

"Why were you surprised to see Ms. Michaels working late?" Sean wasn't about to let her off the spot. His approach was direct, addressing the issue as soon as it came up.

"I was just...surprised."

"Surely you don't think she became head of the catering department without a lot of long nights."

Louise looked befuddled, and if Alex hadn't known the woman better, she might have even felt sorry for her. But there was a belligerent gleam in the blonde's eyes, and she pressed on.

"Oh, come off it! You know who her father is. She could buy this hotel if she wanted to."

Alex felt herself start to freeze up inside. She had suspected Louise resented her, but had no idea it went this deep.

"I'd watch myself if I were you." Sean's voice carried a warning. "You might find yourself looking for another job."

"Not with what I saw the other night. I could call either the *Times* or the *Herald*. I'm sure they'd pounce on it—a juicy little item for their gossip column."

Alex felt sick inside, but kept her face impassive and said nothing. She had a feeling she was about to see a master at work. Louise didn't stand a chance.

"What are you talking about?"

"What do you think?"

"You tell me, then I'll be sure."

"When I walked in that night, she was in your arms."

"Yes, she was. What of it?"

Alex had no idea where this conversation was going.

Louise looked slightly uncertain, now that Sean had admitted to having Alex in what she considered a compromising position. Still, she pressed on.

"You'd been kissing her."

"Had I?"

"Well, she was in your arms—"

"Ms. Michaels has been known to go a long time between meals, has she not?"

Alex began to see a glimmer of where this might be going.

"Am I right?"

Louise was looking down at the floor, seemingly studying her shoes intently. "Yes."

Alex knew it was common knowledge on the floor that she sometimes missed meals, worked straight through lunch and even dinner. Pierre commented on it so often, it was almost a running joke.

"We'd finished our meeting, and she had agreed to see to the first of three private parties I wished to have planned before my wedding day. That *is* what goes on here in the catering department, is it not?"

Louise glanced back up, directly at Sean, her blue eyes wide and hurt. Alex had seen that particular look used with great success on many men.

But Sean was not just any man.

"What you saw, Ms. Hartson, was what happened after Ms. Michaels walked around her desk to see me to her door. She started to feel faint, so I steadied her. Afterward, she was feeling so poorly that she spent the night in a room in this hotel and ordered up a substantial amount of food. You can check with the kitchen if you don't believe me. They have records of the transaction. Now, if this ridiculous accusation is quite finished, I'd like to get back to work. Is that all right with you, Ms. Michaels?"

"Yes." Alex turned her attention to Louise and said, "Please get back to work, Louise. I'd like to see you in my office tomorrow at ten."

"So you can fire me?" A small amount of Louise's normal belligerence was back.

"No. So we can discuss how things are coming along. I've arranged meetings with the other catering assistants, so don't feel that I'm singling you out for anything."

After Louise left the room, Sean said quietly, "You're going to have trouble with that one. I'd fire her and cut your losses."

"I can't. There's no way the department can possibly cover for her. We've all got our hands full. But after the first of the year, I'll let her go."

He wasn't pleased by this, she could tell. And it suddenly touched her that he was concerned for her, wanted to protect her. It had been a long time since she had had someone to watch over her.

Alex placed her fingers on his arm and squeezed gently. Her touch seemed to soothe him, and they continued the last-minute arrangements for the first of the parties.

It was to be something of a bachelor blowout. Sean had reserved one of the main ballrooms and ordered expensive, hearty hors d'oeuvres. No dainty watercress-and-cream-cheese sandwiches for this bunch.

"And you've got us a good bartender."

"The best. Tony knows all the newest drinks, as well as the standards. Do you want me there to supervise things? I usually attend any party I put together, just to make sure things run smoothly."

"If you set it all up and I arrive early, there's no need for you to stay. Besides," he said softly, with the faintest trace of laughter in his voice, "I don't think I'd like you on display in front of this particular group of animals."

"MUFFY BRADFORD! My God, of course!"

"What did you say?" Charlie Michaels looked up over his glasses at his wife of forty-two years. Colleen was fresh out of the shower, wrapped in a white terry robe. They were sharing breakfast coffee on the patio, then he was off to the country club for a round of golf, and Colleen and Beluga would take their daily walk.

And he still thought she looked just as beautiful as the day he'd first seen her.

"She's doing the Bradford wedding."

"So James said. I gathered he was rather proud of her. So was Meredith, come to think of it. Odd."

"Charlie, what I'm trying to tell you is that it has to be Sean Lawton! He's the one! Alex said she felt sorry for the other woman in this whole escapade, and Muffy is the sorriest little thing I've ever seen! Look at this picture!"

She handed him the paper, and he took a look at the picture in the gossip column.

"Nice looking boy. Pity about the girl, though. Looks like a good stiff wind would blow her over."

"Exactly! And Alex can't do anything because if she does, she risks jeopardizing the wedding of the year! Do you realize how much money Constance Bradford must be paying the Biltmore? Oh, my poor Alex!"

"Darling." Charlie reached over and patted his wife's hand, then caught it strongly in his own. "Give poor Mr. Lawton credit for having some brains. He'll realize that our Alex is the right one, not this poor little thing." He studied the picture again. "She looks absolutely miserable."

"What a time for us to be leaving! Oh, Charlie, she needs us!"

He squeezed her fingers again, comfortingly. "I know. It's too bad we can't just fix it like we used to, with an ice-cream cone and a ride on the merry-go-round. But we can't fix things for her now, or make things safe. All we can do is be here for her if she needs us. Why don't I call her today and take her out to lunch?"

"That," Colleen said, "is an excellent idea. Maybe she'll open up a little more to you." She leaned over and kissed him. "I still can't believe I was smart enough to marry you."

He could feel his cheeks growing warm. Though everything the Michaels brothers touched seemed to turn to gold, he had always considered Colleen his greatest treasure.

"ALEX, IT'S YOUR MOTHER on line one."

"I'll take it."

Alex took a deep breath, then picked up the phone.

Calm. Just stay calm.

"Alex? Are you doing anything tonight?"

Oh, no. A date.

"Does this involve a man, Mother?"

"As a matter of fact, darling, a friend of mine has a son who's visiting Los Angeles, and I thought perhaps you could go out with him, just have a drink with him. Nothing too formal. He's staying at the Hyatt down by the airport. You could meet him at that restaurant...Peppercorns, or something like that. I could have him call you."

Alex's first impulse was to refuse. With all the stress she was under, the Bradford wedding, Sean Lawton, Louise's nastiness and her own turbulent emotions, the simple request seemed too much.

But then again, what can it hurt? We're talking about a drink or two, maybe an hour's conversation. Maybe it will get my mind off Sean and this entire fiasco.

And it touched her, the fact that her mother was trying so hard to establish a bond between them.

"All right, Mother. I can make it to the Hyatt by eight."

"Lovely. Alex, he's a charming man. His name is Christopher, but all his friends call him Chip—"

"Wait a minute, I have another call."

"Alex, your uncle. He wants to know if you're free for lunch."

"Tell him yes and to hold just a second." She switched lines. "Mother, I've got Uncle Charlie on the line, so I have to go. I'll meet Chip at eight at the Hyatt in the lobby."

"I'll let him know, Alex. You'll like him."

And Alex, wondering if there was any man on earth who could get her mind off Sean Lawton, picked up the phone and began to talk to her uncle.

"NICE MAN, that Sean," Charlie commented when he got home.

"What do you think? Was I right?" Colleen asked. She was sitting in the middle of their immense den, Beluga standing at attention as she ran a brush through his thick, fluffy black hair.

"He couldn't take his eyes off her. And she was just as bad. I think it's only a matter of time."

"But he's getting married!"

"Something about that just doesn't smell right."

While both Michaels brothers had grown up with money, James had continued to make his the more orthodox way, while Charlie was the brother who relied heavily on his instincts. James saw no reason to invest in a painting unless it was a good tax write-off. Charlie had a house filled with art for no other reason than that he loved to look at it. James had a purebred golden retriever that spent most of its time in a run off the kitchen and thought he belonged to the cook. Charlie had Beluga, who thought he was a human being and would have crawled into bed with them every night had they not bought him a double bed of his own.

"What do you mean?"

"I brought up the wedding just once. He changed the subject. A man in love doesn't do that. Sure, all men are nervous. But when I was getting married to you, I wanted the whole world to know. He's too quiet. I've seen him other places. He has an energy to him. And I only saw that energy directed toward Alex."

"What do we do?"

"As hard as this is going to be, we do nothing." He smiled down at his wife, affection in his clear blue eyes. "Would you have listened to anyone back when we were first together?"

"No, all I wanted to do was be with you."

"You see?"

"But, Charlie—"

"You can't oversee this one, Colleen. We'll just have to trust the two of them to work it out."

"ALEXANDRA, I WANT YOU to know that I feel my daughter is in very capable hands. Everything looks splendid. Now, Sean tells me he's giving a party tomorrow night, one of those bachelor things. Are you taking care of that, as well?"

Constance seemed almost human today, but Muffy looked worse than ever. Pale and listless, she and her mother had been having a tense spat when Alex walked in. It had revolved around the fact that Muffy was losing weight and her wedding dress had already been made. It was a creation fit for a fairy princess, designed out of the finest European lace, being shipped in straight from Belgium in a wooden crate large enough to hold the mannequin. Three seamstresses were also flying in for the wedding. They would sew Muffy into the dress for her big day, to ensure a perfect fit.

"Why don't I call Pierre and see if he can send you up something to eat?" Alex suggested. Muffy truly did not look well, and looking at her, Alex was beginning to feel a horrible sense of guilt. Most of the time, she pushed Sean's crazy plan out of her mind, tried to take one day at a time. When Alex felt her guiltiest, she reminded herself that she was not being intimate with this man, she was not preventing him from getting married and she really wasn't hurting anyone but herself.

She'd voiced her fears to Sean only once, and he had asked her to trust him, as he had before. And the crazy thing was, she did. She believed him when he said he loved her. She had her moments of total insecurity in the middle of the night, and that was when she turned on her bedside lamp and reached under the bed for two or three self-help books. All of them said in a situation such as hers, a woman would be absolutely crazy to agree to anything a swine like this had to offer.

Not that the books listed her specific situation. It was usually listed under the heading "When he wants to date others." There didn't seem to be much in the category of "When he's due to marry another woman by the end of the year."

Still, Alex was much more like her uncle Charlie than her father, and she was starting to play this one by instinct. The most frustrating thing was there weren't exactly any lists she could draw up, and the rule books on this one didn't exist.

"The flowers," Constance was saying. "You're sure this man will do the job? If the flowers aren't perfect, then the whole ceremony is ruined."

"David's an incredibly creative man. He's agreed to be here the day before the wedding and arrange everything."

"And Pierre is making a new cake, you've given me a copy of the menu—" Constance ticked off each item with a relentless organizational ability that Alex, despite her instinctive dislike of the woman, had to admire.

"The music," Muffy said suddenly.

Alex jumped, not used to the sound of her voice.

"It's all taken care of," Constance began carefully, but her daughter interrupted her.

"I want a harpist. Along with the rest of the musicians."

Constance turned toward Alex, a conspiratorial smile on her face. "She's overtired. It's been a long day."

"A harpist."

Alex could feel the tension in the air, and she sensed the argument had nothing at all to do with what kind of music was going to be played at the wedding. Muffy's eyes were enormous in her pale face, and she was biting her lower lip nervously.

And Alex, glancing down, noticed for the first time that the girl's nails were bitten to the quick.

She made up her mind.

"I can find you a harpist easily."

The pent-up fury in Constance's expression was smoothed over so quickly that Alex almost convinced herself she imagined it.

Almost.

There was a lot more going on between mother and daughter than met the casual eye.

It was a tiring meeting, and after Constance and Muffy left, Alex asked Marcy to hold all her calls. She had scheduled a half hour of free time right after the Bradford conference, as she knew these sessions with Constance invariably left her totally exhausted. And as a master—and firm believer—of the catnap, Alex set her alarm, kicked off her shoes and settled herself comfortably on her office couch.

After all, she was going out on an actual date tonight.

Perhaps this man could make her forget Sean Lawton.

Fat chance.

Oh, give him a chance, she chided herself.

Okay. And perhaps Constance Bradford will suddenly reveal that she has the personality of Julie Andrews in The Sound of Music.

Alex, you're very tired.

She started to drift off to sleep.

Stranger things have happened.

"WHAT DO YOU THINK of Louise?" Sean asked, watching as Pierre began to spin caramelized sugar into an intricate web over a plate of meringues.

"Ah, she is like one of these meringues. Full of air and no substance. This dessert looks huge, but you must eat a lot of it to feel full, it is so light. Louise, you would need about fifty of her to make up a woman like Alex."

"Is she a dangerous woman, do you think?"

"She is nasty. And she also has to know Alex has not been pleased with her work. I think that is the most dangerous situation, because she will be like a little animal that is cornered, fighting for its life. She will not care who she hurts. What is the name of that animal?"

"A weasel?" Sean guessed.

"That is the one. Louise is a weasel."

"She fights like a weasel and has all the substance of a meringue. I like that, Pierre. You have quite a way with words."

"Thank you. In my spare time, I work on my novel."

"You write? What kind of novel is it?"

"I hope it will be one of those bestsellers. It is the story of two chefs from Italy, set in an international background. They have dark secrets, there are beautiful women, and everyone eats wonderful food."

"I'm impressed."

"This is none of my business, Sean, but I cannot keep quiet."

"Go ahead."

"I don't want to see Alex get hurt. She has been very good to me."

"I'm not going to hurt her."

"I know you say that. But I hope you mean it. I know what we men can be like. I see the way you look at her. All I am saying is that if Alex is hurt, I may slip something disagreeable into your piece of the wedding cake."

"I understand."

"I think it is a good thing that she is seeing other men."

"What?"

"You did not know? Alex has a date tonight."

Sean's eyes narrowed. "Who?" He didn't like the way his stomach was doing curious little flip-flops. He hadn't felt this vulnerable since the first time he'd looked at a phone and realized he actually had to use it to call a girl.

"Chip. At the Hyatt. He is an old friend of the family. They are meeting for drinks after work, around eight." Pierre carefully kept his total attention on his work.

Oh, my God. Mr. Wonderful, with the family's seal of approval.

"Of course, you would not be intending to make things difficult for Alex, would you?"

"No. No, of course not."

"I WISH I COULD just call Muffy on the phone. Reassure her. She can't be feeling good about this." It was late at night, and Phillip hadn't been able to sleep. He had gone down to the farmhouse kitchen and had been making a cup of herbal tea when Rachel had walked in. She'd been watching an old movie and had been ready to go upstairs to bed, but the sight of Phillip's unhappy face had stopped her.

"You know," Rachel said slowly, "they could probably get you copies of the Los Angeles papers if you asked nicely. Then you could at least follow the gossip columns and have some idea of what's going on."

"I just feel so helpless. I had no idea how frustrating it would be, sitting here and just doing nothing."

"What would you be doing right now, if you weren't stuck here?"

"I'd be thinking up ways to see Muffy. I'd sneak around until we could meet."

"Then," said Rachel, an oatmeal cookie in her hand, "it's a good thing you're stranded here. Didn't you tell me just last night that old Bulldozer Bradford had radar where you were concerned? The jig would be up, the fake wedding would be called off, and they'd probably ship her off to a convent somewhere in Spain."

"You're right."

"There's nothing you can do, Phil. You just have to be patient and wait, and sometimes that's the hardest thing in the world."

"Tell me."

"Tell you what. I've got some sleeping pills in my purse. You won't feel that refreshed when you wake up, but at least they'll help you nod out tonight. And in the morning, I'll see what I can do about getting those newspapers."

"You, Rachel, are too good to be true."

She chuckled. "Ah, but I have a secret angle. Someday, I may ask you to wangle me an introduction to this Sean Lawton. He looks like one yummy guy."

THE LOBBY OF THE HYATT wasn't very crowded, and Alex spotted Chip right away.

She wasn't exactly sure what her mother had in mind for
her in the way of a life partner. Happiness, Alex was sure of
that. Happiness, and perhaps a healthy ration of boredom.

Chip was around six feet, two inches tall. He had sandy,
sun-bleached hair, a handsome face and knew how to dress.
He looked like the consummate boy next door, the type of
guy who would fix your car, take you on long walks, re-
main disgustingly healthy and possess not a single vice.

And he was about as exciting as Richie Cunningham.

Bland. Boring. Vanilla ice cream. Pierre would have put
him on the shelf next to Muffy, both of them pieces of dry
white cake.

She felt not the slightest flare of attraction for this man,
but as Chip clasped her hand in his and smiled down at her,
she recognized the signs.

He was attracted to her.

This could be a long evening.

Throughout the first round of drinks, Alex wondered
what was wrong with her. She'd just finished reading
Women Who Love Too Much, and according to that book's
premise, she was attracted to the wrong sort of man. And
here was Chip, blond, gorgeous Chip, with blue eyes and a
cleft in his chin. So why did she keep thinking of intense
blue-gray eyes, dark hair shot with silver and a physical,
purely male presence that made her go weak at the knees?

After the second glass of white wine, her mind started to
wander.

She was brought back to the present with a start when
Chip laughed, then said, "Cripes, it was funny! Ed had mud
all over him, and when he tried to get back into the canoe,
he tipped it over—"

Cripes? Cripes? *I feel like I'm back in second grade.*

She knew what her mother wanted for her. Security.
Safety. She knew her parents' marriage was not a happy
one, that her father saw other women, that her mother led
her own life. Alex knew exactly what Meredith Michaels had

seen in this man. He would be a good father, a loving husband, a solid companion down the road of life.

And she could have wept, because he did absolutely nothing for her.

She was on her third glass of wine when she was sure she was starting to hallucinate.

Sean Lawton was standing in the doorway, then walking toward their table.

I wanted to see him so badly I conjured him up. Some people see pink elephants, I see Sean Lawton.

When he reached their table, she realized he was no apparition.

"Chip! I can't believe it's you! Good to see you!"

Chip looked up, his expression puzzled. "I'm not sure if—"

"Harvard, wasn't it? The swim team."

"Yale."

"Of course. Yale."

The silence grew uncomfortable, until Sean broke it. "Don't you want me to join you?"

"Of course," said Chip.

"No," said Alex.

Chip looked at her with concern. "Do you want me to—"

She could feel herself flushing, the color crawling up her neck. Trust Sean to embarrass her. "No, no, that's all right. Of course, he can join us."

Chip made a point of sliding over so he was between her and Sean. And Alex, who had been thinking about this man while her date for the evening had been talking about his latest canoe trip, now wished he would go back to the Biltmore, lock himself into the Presidential Suite and throw away the key.

"So, what brings you to Los Angeles, Chip?" The waitress came by, and Sean flagged her down and ordered a

Scotch on the rocks. Alex couldn't help but contrast this with Chip's Perrier with a twist.

She herself was going to need a lot more wine to get through this evening.

"Business. I work for my father."

The two men discussed business for a few minutes, leaving Alex to fiddle with her wineglass and contemplate going to the women's room and never coming back.

Sean was up to something. But what?

"Chip! Perrier? I can't believe it! This, from a man who used to outdrink the entire fraternity."

"Yeah. Those were the days." Chip's eyes had a distinct, nostalgic gleam.

The first time Chip left to go to the men's room, Alex whispered furiously, "You never went to Yale. And how did you know I was here?"

"Big hotels have many little ears."

"I want you to leave. Right now."

"We had an agreement."

"Sean, I'm *not* seeing him, I'm just meeting him for a drink."

"I wouldn't have thought he was your type, Alex."

"How would you know? Come on, Sean, get out of here."

"I wish I could, Alex. But I can't."

"Why not?" She glanced up and saw Chip making his way back to their booth, his blond hair gleaming in the soft light of the lounge.

"I can't stand the thought of you with anyone else but me."

She should have been furious. Instead, his words filled her with a rush of emotion, a fierce satisfaction.

"Hey, Chip, sit down."

"Is that my drink?"

"I ordered it for you while you were gone."

Alex's eyes widened as she began to comprehend the method of Sean's madness. "Sean—"

"Oh, come on, Alex, just a little drink for old times' sake. Then I'll leave you and Chip alone."

One drink turned into three, and a few canoe stories later, six. The next time Chip stood up to go to the men's room, his gait was decidedly unsteady.

"This is not funny," Alex hissed. "You're getting him drunk deliberately!"

"Am I holding the glass to his lips?"

"No, but—"

"I agree, Alex. He's not in very stable condition. I think we should see him up to his room."

She was about to retort when Chip came back up to their table.

"Which way was that bathroom?" he asked, and Sean rose smoothly to his feet.

"Why don't we take you back to your room?" he suggested.

"That might be a good idea," Chip replied.

Many choruses of the Yale fight song later, amid another telling of the infamous Ed-canoeing-in-the-mud story, Chip was finally settled in bed, sleeping peacefully. He looked like a blond angel.

Sean, looking decidedly nonangelic, waited until Chip was deeply asleep before taking Alex's arm and ushering her out of the hotel room.

"You ruined my date." They were in the lobby and halfway out the door before she even spoke to him.

"Come on. He said he had a great time! I've never met a man who was so crazy about canoes."

"Damn it, Sean, you had no right to do this to me."

They were in the parking lot now, and Alex had her key in the lock of her Mercedes when she felt his hand on her elbow. She turned, and that was a mistake, because the space between her car and the next was very close and she could feel his body next to hers.

"You know, my life was perfect until you ruined it."

"I don't think so, Alex. Your life was far from perfect."

She opened her mouth to speak, furious, but his next words silenced her.

"And neither was mine."

He looked at her for a long time, and when he leaned closer, just before he kissed her, she put her hands on his shoulders and tried to wriggle free.

"Don't," he said softly.

Then his lips touched hers, and she was lost.

"It was a rotten thing to do, Alex," he admitted softly, several minutes later. "But I couldn't not do it."

"My *mother* set up the date. He's the son of a friend of hers. We were just meeting over drinks, that was all there was to it."

"But he liked you. I could see that the moment I stepped into the lounge."

"Okay, so he liked me."

"Did you . . . like him?"

"Sure. I mean, I've dated worse."

"You know what I mean."

"Was I attracted to him? No. That privilege is reserved for total boors who break in on my dates and make sure they go straight down the toilet."

He laughed, then kissed her again. "I'll see you tomorrow."

He was halfway across the parking lot when she called out, "Are you always this confident, or is it just me?"

Sean simply smiled.

THE ADVICE IN HER self-help library exhausted, Alex stared at the ceiling that night and ignored Roscoe's snores.

This means war, Sean Lawton. Some party I'll throw you.

Chapter Six

Alex spent most of the day thinking of ways she could get back at Sean for what he had done to her the night before. It hadn't helped that Chip had called from the airport and told her he hadn't enjoyed an evening as much in a long time.

"That Sean," he'd said, admiration in his voice. "Quite a guy."

Men.

But nothing could have prepared her for the disaster awaiting her that evening.

"Alex, we're in trouble. Tony's in the hospital. They think it's diverticulitis."

"Oh, no. Is he all right?"

"Meg said they caught it in time. He's at Cedars right now."

"This is not happening to me," Alex said slowly. "Marcy, what's the name of that school, the one with all the bartenders?"

"American Bartending School."

"What's the name of that guy, the one who runs the school?"

"Jerry. He's great."

"Call him up. We need a bartender."

Moments later Marcy buzzed her back.

"They're closed. His office closed at five. But I know they teach classes somewhere."

"Yeah, but I can't have a student handle this."

"Maybe Pierre knows someone, one of the bartenders from the restaurant. They can't all be working the same night."

"But Tony's special. He's really, really good. I mean, he does all those little things that make a difference."

There was a pause, then Marcy came back with, "Why don't you do it, Alex?"

"I—no. I couldn't."

"Why not? You bartended for a long time. And I bet you were really good."

"Well—"

"As good as Tony."

"Marcy—"

"You can't give this gig to just anyone."

Alex could feel herself starting to relent. "I don't even think I have a tuxedo shirt left."

"Hang on, I'll be right in."

When Marcy came into her office, she was toting a large canvas bag.

"I was going to go out with Peter to this club in Hollywood tonight, and I had this look all planned out, but I can wear something else. We're close enough in size—you'll look just great!"

"What are you talking about?" Alex was beginning to panic. The first of three parties leading up to the wedding of the year, and she didn't have a bartender.

"A dandy. You know, remember Julie Andrews in *Victor/Victoria?* It was a great look. Now, here's the tuxedo shirt...."

EVEN ALEX HAD TO ADMIT she looked great.

The black dinner jacket, trimmed in rhinestones, fit with the addition of shoulder pads. The icy-white, ruffled tuxedo shirt was a bit tight and tucked into a pair of black trousers with a satin ribbon running down each outside leg. But the ultimate touch was the large, plushy fur coat—fake, Marcy assured her. It was like being smothered by Beluga.

"I don't like the shirt. It pulls across your boobs."

Alex glanced down. Marcy was right. The shirt was the only part of the outfit so far that didn't look right.

"I've got it," Marcy said suddenly. "This is a slightly formal event, right?"

"They'll be coming from work, so they'll be wearing suits."

"Don't wear the shirt."

"Marcy, I don't know—"

"Don't wear the shirt. Trust me, Alex, I know clothes. Just button the jacket and you won't even need it."

When Marcy was done with her, Alex studied herself in the full-length mirror in her bathroom. She looked incredible. Like no bartender she'd ever seen. What made the outfit shift from formal to incredibly sexy was the subtraction of the shirt.

But it worked. And with the party starting at eight, and no other bartender in sight that she trusted the way she trusted Tony, what was she supposed to do?

She had other thoughts. She wondered what Sean would do when he found out she was going to be attending his bachelor bash. The thought of his displeasure was incredibly satisfying.

She was certain Sean wasn't going to be happy about this, but if she had learned one lesson in her years of catering, it was that the show must go on.

Marcy, insisting Alex needed something around her neck, had fastened a black velvet ribbon with a sparkling rhinestone pin. Alex had several pairs of shoes in her closet, and Marcy selected a pair of black leather flats.

Marcy also gave her an antique silk purse to stash her lipstick in, and fastened a rhinestone stickpin to the lapel of the jacket. "Insurance, in case someone gets drunk and tries to get a little fresh, you know?"

Marcy then took on Alex's hair, braiding it back with the silver ribbon she'd planned to wear as a headband.

"Now, go do your makeup. Light face, dark eyes and lips. We're going for the sort of sick-is-chic look, you know what I mean?"

As Alex did her makeup, Marcy drilled her on the drinks.

"I'll never remember them all."

"It'll come back to you. What's in a Tequila Sunrise?"

"Tequila, orange juice, grenadine. And a cherry."

"A Sunset?"

"Blackberry brandy instead of the grenadine."

"I'm impressed. What about a California driver?"

"Vodka, orange juice and grapefruit juice."

"Good. No, not the mauve. Here, try this claret gloss. Keep it for the evening. A wine spritzer—no, these guys aren't into that. How about a Rusty Nail?"

The drill continued as they left Alex's office and headed down toward the ballroom where the party was to be held.

"Sloe Gin Fizz."

"Sloe gin, sweet and sour, soda and a cherry."

"Fuzzy Navel."

"Vodka, orange juice and peach schnapps."

Marcy stayed by her side, reviewing drinks, even as Alex began to set up the bar.

"Velvet Hammer."

"White crème de cacao, triple sec and cream."

Marcy was still whispering drinks to her as Sean walked in the large double doors.

"A Russian Quaalude."

"Stoli's, Kahlua, Bailey's and Frangelico."

"You got it, Alex. Good luck."

And with that, Marcy smiled and stepped back slightly.

"You look great. Kill 'em."

Unless someone kills me first. Marcy was already almost out the door, and Sean was walking straight toward Alex. She could tell by the look in his eyes that he was not at all pleased to see that she was going to be attending his bachelor bash.

"What are you doing behind the bar?"

"Tony—the bartender I had hired for tonight—is in the hospital. They think it's diverticulitis. I couldn't get anyone else on such short notice, so I decided I'd do it."

"There isn't anyone else in this entire hotel who could bartend tonight?"

"There's no one else who's as good as Tony." *Or me,* she added silently, her chin lifting just a fraction. Alex had prided herself on being the best bartender possible, and she was surprised how suddenly it mattered to her whether she did this job or not.

She could see from the expression on Sean's face that he was going to try to veto this plan as quickly as he could, so she jumped back into the fray. It might be a very good thing for this man to realize he couldn't always get his own way.

"After all, unless you did it behind my back, you didn't request a giant cake, so I know there won't be any naked girls running around. And studies show that men just love a female bartender."

He sighed deeply, his fingers raking his thick, dark hair back from his forehead. "I know. Alex, I just don't think you should do this."

Realization came so suddenly that she was surprised she hadn't sensed what was really going on. *He's jealous. He asked me not to see any other men, and now, if I tend bar, I'll be in the middle of a ballroom full of them. How wonderful.* Another attribute of the modern man—or at least of the modern men *she* had been dating until her self-proclaimed sabbatical—was his casual acceptance of open dating. Or, as it had been said to her more than once, "Hey, babe, you do your thing, and I'll do mine. And if we meet, it's beautiful, you know what I mean?''

Jealousy, like lust, was something that had been in short supply in her life. Until Sean. It struck her that she was intensely, fiercely *glad* that he wasn't a man to do anything halfway.

And there was no way he could deflect the number of men he had invited. He'd been able to handle Chip, but what about a roomful of men?

The possibilities were endless.

''Will you do something for me?''

His question brought her back to the present moment. ''Sure.'' *Why not? I've already thought about agreeing to your other suggestion, and so if I'm not certifiable by now, what's another request?*

''Let Pierre send someone up.''

''All right, I'll just go powder my nose.''

There was a phone in the bathroom, and Alex dialed Pierre's extension with record speed.

''Pierre?''

''Yes.''

''Send Carl.''

''*Chérie,* you are a cruel woman.''

''He's jealous.''

''Of what? You, in your little tuxedo without a blouse, among all those men tonight? How silly of him.''

''Is Marcy there with you?''

''She's eating one of my truffles right now.''

''Tell her thanks.''

''With pleasure, *ma coeur.* Carl is on the way.''

Carl was a blue-eyed blond, with typical surfer good looks that were barely restrained in a tuxedo. He didn't look too intimidated by Sean, and Alex guessed that Pierre must have given him some inside instructions as to this particular job.

''Hey, dude, let's party.''

Alex saw the tiniest bit of worry in Sean's eyes and had to bite her inner lip hard to keep from laughing.

"Are you familiar with most standard drinks?"

"Sure. Whiskey and water, Scotch and soda—those aren't too hard."

Carl, Alex decided, was priceless.

Sean hesitated, then said quickly, "Make me a Melon Ball."

Carl, with unerring inaccuracy, went straight for the rum.

"Vodka, Carl," Alex whispered, just loud enough so Sean could hear.

"Oh, yeah, I don't know why I did that, my mind just blanked out, you know what I mean? Okay, vodka, and then orange juice, right?"

Alex nodded her head, looking as if she was pleased he was catching on.

Carl set the highball glass up on the spill rail, looking pleased with himself.

"Where's the Midori?" Sean asked quietly.

"Right here." Carl hefted the liqueur bottle up, tossed it so that it turned in midair, caught it and quickly poured a scant half ounce in the glass. Just enough so that it was filled to the brim and impossible to pick up.

He caught Sean's disapproval, then glanced at the glass.

"Oh. Sorry. Here, I'll just dump some of it out—"

"Not on the fresh ice, Carl! Here, over on the side."

"Whoa, what was I thinking? No, no, I've got it now. Call me another one, man."

"Let's see you do a gin and tonic."

"Nice well you got here, dude. I'm impressed. Stoli's, Tanqueray, Bacardi—"

"Where's the lime?"

"Oh, yeah! A garnish, of course."

"Make me a Ramos Fizz," Sean said. His jaw was beginning to tighten up. Alex glanced at her watch. Thirteen minutes till showtime. Guests would start arriving any minute.

Carl, bless his heart, looked at Sean blankly, a lock of sun-bleached hair falling over his tanned forehead.

"You're kidding me, man. That's a drink?"

"A Ramos Fizz," Sean said slowly, enunciating each syllable.

Carl just stood there. Then he turned to Alex. "Help me out on this one, Alex."

She stepped behind the bar. Without a second's hesitation, Alex placed a wineglass with some ice cubes in it on the speed rail. Then she reached for the container of the small portable blender, threw in ice, gin, cream, sweet-and-sour mix and a few dashes of orange-flower water.

Inside the small portable refrigerator, she found an egg, expertly separated the white from the yolk and threw the white into the blending cup. Then, while the drink was blending, she dumped the ice out of the wineglass, then strained the contents into the wineglass and topped it off with some soda.

The silence was deafening.

"Well," said Alex, after a short, yet pregnant pause, "I'm sure there's some paperwork waiting for me somewhere." As she started to leave the room, she heard Carl telling Sean about the last party he had bartended and how he was an expert at arranging kegs of beer.

"Alex, wait."

She turned, almost at the door of the Emerald Room. Sean was hosting a rather large party tonight, and the room looked especially elegant. All the banquet rooms off the Galleria were done in a Spanish-Italian Renaissance architecture, with columns, friezes, crystal-laced chandeliers and mythological figurines. She wondered if Constance Bradford, had she insisted on having her way and controlling this little gathering, would have insisted all the men attend this bachelor blowout in Renaissance garb.

An evening of bartending and watching some of the city's most powerful men in tights and tunics would have been an absolute blast. But it would be good enough seeing all of them in their elegant business suits, mixing them drinks and watching Sean's reaction.

It was just what he deserved, after last night and the fiasco with Chip.

She was just feeling frisky enough to enjoy all of this. After all, no matter what Sean said, he still had Muffy waiting in the wings. Why not let him get a taste of what it was like to feel a little insecure, to not be sure whether things were going to turn out the way he wanted them to?

There was only so much that Lawton willpower could accomplish. Suddenly Alex was quite sure she was going to find this entire evening highly entertaining—and revealing.

"Yes?"

He strode quickly up beside her, his hands thrust in his pants pockets, a displeased expression on his face. This was a man not used to being thwarted. "Carl's not going to work. Is there anyone else Pierre can send up?"

As if on cue, a tall, lanky blond man entered the Emerald room.

"Sean Lawton! You sure sprung a quick one on all of us! I didn't even know you were seeing Muffy!"

Alex quickly extricated herself from Sean and his guest, then walked over to the bar and smiled at Carl.

"You're wasting your time at the Biltmore, Carl. Have you ever considered going into acting?"

He grinned. "I'm taking acting classes on the side. I was with Jeff Corey, now I'm with this other guy, he's pretty good. And my agent is working on getting me a part on a soap."

Only in L.A. "Well, you did a great job here, and I appreciate it. Now get going before he changes his mind."

"I'm history, Alex."

Within seconds, Sean was back at the bar. Three other men had walked in, and a group of them were talking and laughing by the door. In a matter of minutes, they would want drinks, and Alex was counting on Sean just giving in.

"Where did Carl go?"

"Sean, he couldn't handle a party like this. Do you think I want that kind of news to get back to *my* boss? I couldn't have let him mess things up."

He frowned. Sean was smart, and knew he was backed into a corner. However, in a typically masculine fashion, he wasn't going to give up gracefully.

"All right. You can tend bar, but just until Pierre sends up someone who can replace you. And—damn it, Alex, what happened to your shirt?"

"What shirt?"

The muscles in his jaw tensed again. "What exactly do you have on underneath that jacket?"

"You mean, besides a black lace camisole? Nothing."

The look in his blue-gray eyes was everything she had hoped for—and more. This was a man who knew how most men's minds worked—and he didn't want her to be the object of some of their more spectacular fantasies.

"*I'll* get behind that bar and see to things until you can find yourself a shirt. Go on."

"But, Sean, that's why I wore this pin. Nothing's going to come undone. That would be most unprofessional." She'd moved her hand to the front of the jacket, to the deep vee of the lapels, where you could just see the faintest shadow of cleavage. His eyes followed the movement, and their color deepened.

Highly entertaining was the understatement of the year.

"Alex, we have to—"

"Hey, pretty lady. How about a rum and Coke? What kind of rum do you have?"

"Only the best for you," Alex replied without thinking. She'd bantered with the best of them during her years behind the bar. "How's Bacardi?"

"Nice. Very nice. Make it a double." The expression in the man's dark eyes left Alex in no doubt that he wasn't just referring to the rum.

As Alex quickly mixed highballs, she could see that Sean was stuck. He wanted to go phone Pierre and ask him to send him someone else, but he didn't want to leave her alone with four of his friends. She sensed he was almost ready to make a dash for the phones when another wave of men entered the banquet room and headed straight for the bar.

"Hey, Sean, only the best for your buddies, right?"

The look in his eyes . . .

She'd forgotten just how entertaining bartending could be.

"Darling, make me a Tanqueray and tonic."

"A vodka martini, and could I have two olives, sweetheart?"

"Honey, I'd like a Climax."

The look in Sean's eyes was murderous. And Alex, the woman who never dared, made out lists and religiously read self-help books in an attempt to figure out the rules of the mating game, began to improvise.

"Would you like me to make that a Screaming Climax?"

"Alex, could I speak to you for a minute?" There was a dangerous glint in his eyes.

"Wait a minute, Sean." The man was from Texas, judging from his accent and the languorous way he moved his big body. "She really is a bartender! I thought you just hired someone this pretty as part of the decorations, if you know what I mean. Now, honey, what was that last one? It sounded *mighty* interesting."

"A Screaming Climax. You just add vodka."

"Alex—"

The Texan threw back his head and laughed uproariously, then, once he calmed down, said, "Toss that vodka right in. You make me feel reckless, little lady."

Sean was about to say something when another wave of guests descended on the bar. Alex only had time for a quick glimpse of his face to know, with a feeling of dread certainty, that she was going to end up paying for this mischief sooner or later.

"SEAN, YOU CAN'T just spend all your time here at the bar. Parties are for mingling, and you're the host. Get out there and mingle."

"They all end up coming to the bar sooner or later. I can talk to them here as well as I can out there."

She hid her smile as she reached for a lime and began to cut it into wedges. Sean had certainly stocked enough in the way of wines, liquor and liqueurs. Even some imported beers. The party was in full swing, the banquet room was crowded, but there was a lull at the bar. Typical. Parties usually picked up toward the end, with everyone wanting one last drink.

Alex watched the crowd carefully. One of the most important things she'd learned while bartending was to make sure not to serve anyone past their limit. There wasn't going to be any problem at this party, though. There was plenty of food to counteract the effects of the alcohol, and none of Sean's male friends had made it a point to overindulge.

As the lime juice made contact with the small paper cuts in her hands, she caught her breath sharply.

"What's wrong?"

"Nothing. My hands are full of paper cuts, and I just got some lime juice in them. I'll live."

She cut more garnishes in silence, then said softly, "I think the party's going really well, Sean. What do you think?"

"I think you're quite a bartender." His tone wasn't grudging. There was respect in his voice and that certain kind of admiration that comes when something brand-new is discovered in a person you thought you knew pretty well.

"Thank you. I try my best."

"I can see why you've made it to the top of your profession."

"Thank you." She made a Scotch and soda for one of the guests. The man thanked her politely, then tried to wangle her phone number out of her. Alex evaded his question without damaging his male pride, and when the man left the bar to rejoin the group he had been with before, Alex could feel Sean's gaze on her face.

"Alex, I—"

"Sean, there you are! Get over here. Carter and I haven't seen you all evening. Though I can see why you'd want to hang out at the bar." The man who addressed this comment to Sean looked like the quintessential Ralph Lauren model.

This time, Sean couldn't avoid his guest. With just the slightest amount of detectable reluctance, he left the bar.

Alex, garnishes finished, well liquors and jockey boxes restocked, let her gaze sweep over the assemblage of men gathered in the Emerald Room. There were women who would have died to have the opportunity to meet these men, most of them single, all of them successful. It was definitely the equivalent of an E-ticket ride at Disneyland in the world of dating.

Nothing Alex had ever read in any of her self-help books could have prepared her for this evening. The closest heading she could remember was something like, "Try to see the man of your dreams in as many different settings as possible." But she'd done rather well. She'd learned that Sean, when it came to love, was just like any other man. A man could wield tremendous power, could buy and sell and make the deal of the century, but when it came to love, he was simply a man.

He didn't like her being here, the lone woman in a group of handsome, successful men. Now, as she thought of his wedding, as she thought of having to watch Muffy Bradford walk up the aisle, Alex began to reconsider the allowances she'd been making for Sean.

Who did he think he was, telling her not to pay attention to any other men? And when would she have a chance like this again? And, best of all, for some perverse reason, she was getting a tremendous amount of sheer pleasure at seeing him thwarted in getting something he wanted.

I'm not a building, Sean Lawton. You can't make one of your deals with me.

"Hi, babe." The man standing in front of the bar looked like a young Nick Nolte, all blond hair and muscles, with the bluest eyes. Attractive. Very attractive.

"Hi, yourself. What can I get you?"

"Behind the bar, you mean?"

"Mmm...yeah." She could see Sean out of the corner of her eye, and she could feel his presence.

It was volatile.

This man was not a happy camper.

"How about a shot of tequila?" said Nick, as she thought of him.

"Good choice. I like a man who likes tequila." A corny line, but it *always* worked.

"You do?"

"A double or a single?"

"Aw, why not. Give me a double."

He *was* cute. He didn't stir her up the way Sean did, but maybe this was what she needed. Someone to break that self-imposed sabbatical. Someone to show Sean that she wasn't just waiting for him to walk in so that she could jump up, roll over, play dead.

Be daring, a sneaky little voice whispered in her ear. *Look what he did to you last night.*

He's going to be furious, the voice of reason shot back.

The battle of the brains, right against left, instinct versus reason, began.

Do it.

You'll pay for it.

So what. I'd like to see him lose that self-assurance. He's always so much in control.

Be honest, Alex, you'd like to see him lose it completely.

Okay, so maybe I would. So what?

You may get more than you bargained for....

"So, you doing anything after the party?"

An electric silence. She could *feel* Sean, sense that he was within earshot, that he would hear her reply, that whatever she said would play a crucial part in what happened next.

"Nope."

Go for it!

Oh, no.

"How about a quiet dinner at Bernard's? I'd like to get to know you ... away from here, someplace we could really talk."

Come on, come on!

You'll be sor-ree....

"I'd really like that."

"I'll go make reservations. Think you'll be off in about an hour and a half?"

Don't do it, Alex!

"I know I will."

Whoopee!

"All right." He was giving her a totally male, assessing look.

She met his gaze, then smiled slowly.

Don't do it, Alex! It'll be the nail in the coffin.

Ah, why not? If you're going to do it, go all the way.

"You have excellent taste—"

"Steven. But everyone calls me Steve."

"Steve. I'm Alex. Bernard's is a very romantic place."

"I hope so." There was a devilish glint in his blue eyes as he turned and walked toward the main door of the Emerald Room.

She reached for another lime, as there was no one at the bar and she wanted something, anything, to do with her hands so she wouldn't have to meet Sean's eyes.

There was a palpable chill in the air.

"You're not going out with him."

"I beg your pardon?"

"We made a deal."

"A deal I'm beginning to think wasn't such a good one."

"Don't do this, Alex."

"Tell me why you think you have any rights at all when it comes to what I will and will not do."

Wow, that was pretty good. What self-help book was that from?

But Alex was winging it and enjoying herself immensely.

"I won't let you do this."

"What are you planning on doing, dragging me out of this room forcibly? Locking me up?" She met his gaze, and it was frigid. "This is the twentieth century, Sean, not the fourteenth. Women aren't possessions anymore, even when they do choose to get married. Are you planning on treating Muffy this way? Does she know what you have in store for her?"

There was a perverse little demon riding her. She'd believed she could handle this whole thing, but the thought of Sean with another woman was more than she could bear. She wanted to hurt him the way he was hurting her.

"That's enough."

"Oh, I don't think so. The deal's off, Mr. Lawton. I want that part of this discussion to be perfectly clear."

"You're destroying things, Alex."

"Am I?" She didn't know where all this anger was coming from. She had sat up at night, wondering what was going to happen, making all sorts of allowances for Sean. Now, taking a good look at where things were going, she decided to take a stand.

But her emotions were still in conflict.

Go for it. You're really getting to him.

But he asked you to trust him....

But he's marrying Muffy—

But you love him....

That one caught her off guard and she stared at Sean, sure that the strangest facial expression of all time was revealing to him what she'd just admitted to herself.

"Tell me," she said, and when her voice quavered, she stopped long enough to compose herself. "Tell me exactly what it is that we have. And don't start up with all that lust stuff. It's not enough, Sean."

"It's all there is."

"Not for me. I need more. I need to know that you'll be there for me no matter what, that I can count on you, lean on you. I'm so damned sick of people I can't depend on—"

She stopped, suddenly horrified by what she'd revealed.

He was looking at her, as if trying to fit together the pieces of an intricate puzzle.

And, of course, at the exact moment when they might have been able to pull everything together, three men descended on the small bar.

"Darling, how about a refill—"

"A Tequila Sunrise—"

"Just Perrier, with a twist—"

Alex immersed herself in the drinks, chatting, laughing, smiling. Sean, looking like he wanted to upend the entire bar, stalked off to the opposite end of the large room.

Stalemate. Well, you got what you wanted.

Did I?

She wasn't sure.

"WONDERFUL PARTY, wasn't it?" Alex said brightly as she surveyed the empty Emerald Room. She and Sean were the only people left in the large banquet room, the rest of the guests had left, and she had five minutes to make it to Bernard's. She'd unbraided her hair, and it cascaded down her back in shining waves. With the thick, plushy fur coat around her, she was dressy enough for the four-star restaurant.

Sean simply looked at her, a purely male anger in his eyes. "Don't do this, Alex."

Oh, Sean, it's for my own protection. You scare me.

"I'll see you in the morning."

"Well," he said, sounding resigned, "At least let me help you with your coat and walk you to the door."

The tiny, secret part of her woman's heart was upset that he wasn't going to put up more of a struggle.

"All right."

He walked behind her, holding the coat, and at the same time she moved her arms behind her so that he might help her into it.

Too late, she realized he'd trapped her.

The coat, voluminous and fluffy, came down over her head in a smooth swish, and at the same time she felt strong arms lift her up, then thump her over hard shoulder bone.

The breath left her body in a painful rush, and then, furious, she began to struggle.

"Put me down, you rat! Right now! Down!"

In answer, she felt a large hand come stinging down on her buttocks, and she was shocked speechless.

He was walking swiftly now, and she began to struggle. Her heart was pounding, the small, secret woman's part utterly *furious*. Her mouth was dry, and she couldn't seem to form the words necessary to tell the world that she was in the hands of a madman.

By the time she did, it was too late.

They were in the elevator now, and frustrated tears filled Alex's eyes as she realized it wasn't stopping at any of the floors.

Which could only mean one thing.

They were in the private elevator that went directly to the Presidential Suite, the top two floors of the Biltmore, its most luxurious accommodation.

And the temporary lair of one Sean Lawton.

Chapter Seven

He set her down on the bed with a resounding thump.

Alex, still tangled within the folds of Marcy's fur coat, had heard the key scrape in the lock, and that meant she was locked in the Presidential Suite with Sean.

As she struggled up out of the fluffy black fur and brushed her hair out of her face, she saw Sean slip the key into his pocket.

"You," she said slowly, with as much dignity as she could muster, "are a pig."

He said nothing, simply looked at her, his beautiful blue-gray eyes revealing none of his feelings.

"I'm getting out of here and going downstairs to Bernard's."

"Just try it."

Furious, Alex jumped to her feet and walked briskly to the door. Locked. She rattled the knob, then began to really twist it. Finally, frustrated beyond endurance, she turned toward Sean, her temper raw.

"Give me that key."

"Are you going to go out with Steve?"

"That...is...none...of...your...business!"

"No." His jaw was set, the blue eyes cold now.

"This is not the fourteenth century—"

"You were the one who gave me the idea."

She could remember her taunting words.

"What are you planning on doing, dragging me out of this room forcibly? Locking me up?"

Me and my big mouth.

What would any of the authors of her self-help books tell her to do now? "What to do when he goes berserk and locks you in a hotel suite with him when you want to go out with another man." Nope, that wasn't exactly something that was covered in detail.

You were the one who wanted to see him lose control. Well, now you know.

"I really, really hate you."

"I really don't care. Take off your jacket."

"What!"

"Just a little insurance in case you think about escaping. There's no way you'll call anyone for help if you're up here in your underwear."

She glanced wildly at the phone and would have started toward it if he hadn't stopped her with a look.

"Take off your jacket. Or I'll do it for you."

"Sean, you can't be—"

"I want to see that black camisole. I've been thinking about it all night."

Me and my great, big stupid mouth.

That same mouth totally incapable of any coherent reply, Alex stared at Sean, still not believing he could be serious.

"What if I said," she began nervously, "that I would forget this entire incident and go straight down to my car and go directly home?"

"Too late. Off. Now."

She stared at him.

He took a step toward her.

Her hands flew to the rhinestone stickpin, her fingers fumbling as she began to unfasten it.

He leaned back against the wall by the bed, hands in his pockets, a slow, arrogantly masculine smile appearing on his face.

She unbuttoned the first button of Marcy's black jacket.

"Sean, I really think we need to—"

"Come on."

The second of four buttons was unfastened, and her mouth went dry at the thought of Sean seeing her in her underwear. It was extremely nice underwear, a black silk, lace-trimmed camisole and tap pants, but it was still underwear. And he was still the most devastating man she'd ever met.

She unfastened the third button, then the fourth. The jacket was completely unbuttoned, but it still concealed her from his gaze.

"Sean, I cannot believe that a civilized man—"

"I'm tired of being civilized. Take it off."

Their eyes locked and held, the only sound the ticking of a clock somewhere in the penthouse. She couldn't look away, his gaze was so compelling. And Alex realized, now that they were completely alone, how strong the attraction between them was. Now, up in this suite, there was no one watching them, no one to suspect there was any sort of feeling between them. And she knew this man could open her up emotionally in ways no other man had ever even come close to. It was crazy, it made absolutely no sense, but her body was way ahead of her mind, her instincts were racing ahead of any logic she possessed.

It was simply there. Pure energy, intense sexuality. An incredibly compelling attraction that was so strong it hurt.

Finally, after what seemed endless minutes, she looked away.

He knows.

Somewhere, somehow, her fury was swiftly turning to the strongest feeling of arousal she'd ever experienced.

Hadn't she thought about this? Fantasized about being alone with him?

So easy. No one would ever have to know. A few hours, the privacy of a suite, the key turned securely in the lock. A chance to see how good it would be with Sean, who takes one look at me and does more with that look than most men are capable of doing with their entire bodies. I want to know how it would be with him. I want to know....

This man, this wildly infuriating, complex, stubborn, blatantly-masculine-and-proud-of-it man was like a blast of dynamite to her libido. In an age of men who dated, married and fathered children casually, in an age when divorce was the solution to the pettiest of problems, this man was like a throwback to a different time, when men took what they wanted and knew their actions would merit consequences they were prepared to face.

And conquer.

Yet...yet in the strangest of ways, her instincts were screaming at her that this was a man who would take care of the woman he loved, even if the arrangements were a little unorthodox, at best.

"Off, Alex. Now."

She released her jacket, shrugged out of it and let it slip down off her shoulders to fall at her feet.

"Now the slacks."

They joined the jacket on the floor, and, suddenly embarrassed, she swept her hair over her shoulders so that she might have some sort of covering, no matter how ineffectual. The silk was so thin, whisper-sheer, not any sort of protection at all from that blatantly masculine gaze.

"Push your hair back over your shoulders."

She looked up at him, fighting against the temptation to beg. She would never do that. She felt as if she would die before she let him know how discomfiting this was.

"Come here."

This is it.

Swallowing hard, she walked slowly toward him until she was standing in front of him. She knew he was looking at her silk-clad body, and she resisted the urge to look up into his face until the desire to do so was so compelling she couldn't not do it.

The look in his eyes destroyed her.

If eyes could worship, his were doing so. Burning into her, letting her know he was pleased by what he saw.

Feeling strangely empowered, she whispered, "Is it—am I like you imagined?"

"Better."

His arms came around her, warm and hard, and he pulled her up against him, holding her. His body was incredibly warm through the silk against her skin, and she moved closer to that warmth and sighed, tension leaving her body.

They stood that way for a long time, Sean simply holding her, until he kissed her. She knew the instant before he lifted her chin with his fingers, and she closed her eyes and tried to steel herself against the onslaught of feeling.

It was useless. She felt like tinder catching fire as the kiss deepened. His lips were warm and firm, leading, coaxing, caressing. Then demanding. And she wanted him in a way that was utterly foreign to her, in a way she had wanted no other man in her life.

All rational thought left her as she moved closer, touched the warmth of his cheek, curled her fingers around the strength of his shoulders, then his neck. She could feel his hands against the small of her back, pressing her closer and closer....

Then holding her away from him, the movement so smooth and steady it took her a moment to realize the kiss had been broken.

He held her for several minutes, and she could feel his heart racing. Alex gently placed her palm against his chest, and the muscles clenched sharply. He caught her fingers and kissed her palm.

"Let's get in bed."

Her body tensed, and he was quick to reassure her. "Nothing's going to happen, Alex. I give you my word. I just want to keep you close for a while."

She could have pointed out to him that Steve had probably left Bernard's by now, that she was too emotionally exhausted to even contemplate seeing another man, let alone carrying on a coherent conversation with him. But the truth was, she wanted to be close to this man for a short time, away from prying eyes and the need to conceal what she truly felt for him.

She could admit it to herself, but not to him. Not yet. If she did, she felt as if she would be totally vulnerable, totally exposed. She'd keep this new knowledge of the way she felt about Sean to herself just a little longer.

"Come on, baby, I'll tuck you in." The endearment wouldn't have sounded right from any other man but Sean, and Alex knew she was falling fast, into a whirlpool of intense feeling and emotions she seemed powerless to resist. They frightened her, these emotions. But the thought of never feeling them again frightened her even more.

He lifted her into his arms so easily, with a masculine grace that made it seem he had held her in his arms this way many times before. She was frightened for an instant, frightened of so much power, and her fingers curled around the strength in his shoulders, needing his support. As Sean walked toward the bed, Alex softly rested her cheek against his.

There was such tenderness in this man, as well as stubbornness and pride. Held securely in his arms, she felt cherished. Even loved.

He sat her down on the big bed, then pulled back the covers and helped her in. When he tucked the sheet and quilted bedspread around her carefully, Alex felt as if she were infinitely precious to him.

"Are you hungry? Did you eat dinner?"

She shook her head.

"Do you want to order something from room service?"

She shook her head again. These new feelings and everything that had transpired tonight had exhausted her.

Linking her fingers around his neck, she gently pulled his head down to hers.

"Can we sleep? Just a little bit?"

"Anything you want."

She closed her eyes as she heard him slipping off his clothes. Even as tired as she was, a flare of painful excitement slipped through her. Then she heard the bedside lamp click off, and he was beside her, so close . . .

It took her a few seconds to realize he wasn't going to touch her, and she was thankful, not knowing what would happen if he did.

Alex reached out in the darkness until she found his hand. She grasped it firmly, linked fingers with him, hers cool against the warmth of his. With a sigh, she turned her flushed face against the cool cotton of the pillowcase and slept.

SEAN LAY IN BED, listening to the sound of Alex's deep breathing. Face-to-face with his deepest feelings, he thought of what he was putting Alex through.

He'd come close to making love to her, so close to forgetting every rational thought he'd ever entertained about their relationship. They were mature adults. They could handle this. And the topper—if she couldn't handle this relationship and keep it under control, he could.

Hah.

It wasn't like him. Not at all. First, destroying her date with Chip. Then tonight . . . This wasn't like him at all.

None of this is like you.

He'd never met a woman who stirred his feelings as deeply as Alex did. He couldn't stay away from her office, couldn't resist the times he wanted to pick up the phone just to hear the sound of her voice.

He'd never met a woman before that he hadn't felt completely in control around. In his heart of hearts, he had longed to feel more. Now, in the midst of loving Alex, he knew he'd drastically underestimated what those feelings would be like.

He had no doubt that their relationship—and where it was going—was always on her mind. Because it was always on his. He felt as if he knew her, knew what went on in her mind and sometimes even how she felt.

Alex murmured in her sleep, then rolled over, jostling her body against his. Sean shifted his arm so it was securely around her, feeling her warmth, the softness of her skin, and smelling the spicy fragrance she always wore.

This was deeper than anything he'd ever felt. He was in love with this woman, over the moon. And no matter how it unnerved him, there was no going back.

WHEN SHE WOKE, she saw him standing by the window, staring out at the dark skyline. He was dressed in a pair of dark blue, silk pajama bottoms, his feet bare. She watched him, enjoying the sight of him during such a private moment.

His shoulders were tensed, and she realized he was staring out the window but not really seeing anything. The line of his back was beautiful, but there was something so very vulnerable about him. As if there were moments when that tremendous strength faltered, when he himself felt vulnerable.

He was simply beautiful. And for this short time, inside these walls, he was hers in a way he would probably never be again.

"Sean?" Her voice was quiet in the silent room.

He straightened, his posture changing so subtly that she might have imagined the initial way she'd seen him.

He sat down next to her on the bed.

"Do you feel better?"

"Much better."

"Alex, I'm not proud of what I did this evening, and I'm not going to try and make any excuses—"

She linked her hand with his, lifted it to her lips and placed a kiss on the back of his hand.

"Don't apologize. You didn't hurt me."

He looked at her for a long moment, her face shadowed in the soft light of the suite. Then he said, "Hungry?"

"Yes."

"We'll order up."

They moved one of the tables right next to a large window, and called down to room service. Later, over crisp roasted Peking duck with fresh egg fettuccine and plum sauce, grilled swordfish with ginger and Szechuan peppers, and medallions of lamb with fresh thyme and sweet garlic, they talked very carefully, skirting the more painful issues.

But later, back in bed with chocolate-covered strawberries and a bottle of champagne, Alex finally spoke from her heart.

"I can't go through with it, Sean. I can't watch you marry another woman. I'm not as sophisticated as you seem to think I am."

He took another sip of champagne, watching her over the rim of the slender flute.

"If I asked you to trust me again, even after tonight, could you do it?"

"I want to. But I'm confused." She swallowed against the sudden tightness in her throat. "Sean, why are you taking part in this marriage if you don't love her?"

He was silent for a time before he spoke, and Alex knew he was weighing his words carefully.

"Alex, if I told you it had everything to do with loyalty and nothing to do with love, and if I told you that once the wedding is over, nothing will stand in the way of our being together, would you believe me?''

Slowly, so slowly, she nodded her head. "I would."

He looked up at the ceiling then, and she could see the small muscle working in his jaw. She touched his face, and his eyes were instantly riveted to hers.

"I don't deserve you," he said quietly. "I don't know what the hell I did to have you walk into my life, but I thank the gods every day that you did."

She moved slowly across the bed until she was nestled in the crook of his shoulder, her head against his chest. She could hear the rapid beating of his heart, feel the warmth of his skin, smell the distinct scent that was his alone. It soothed her.

"You scare me," she whispered.

"I do?"

She nodded her head.

"Why?"

"You make me— I feel so out of control around you. I never lose my temper, I never yell at people, I've never felt so many different feelings before I met you."

She was silent for a time, then whispered, "I don't like feeling out of control."

His arms were warm around her as he pulled her closer against him. "Then let me be in control for both of us, Alex. Nothing is going to happen to you, I'm not going to hurt you. I promise."

He turned off the light, and they lay in the big bed together, watching the first rays of sunlight start to streak the night sky.

"Are you crying?" he asked suddenly, so softly. "Alex, darling, don't cry. We'll be fine." He turned his head and kissed her then, his lips warm and reassuring against her cheek.

"I'm so happy." The words were muffled against his neck. "I'm just so happy."

"CHARLIE, I'M SO HAPPY we're going home."

"Still thinking about her, aren't you?"

"I haven't thought about much else. They're perfect together. Everything you've told me about Sean, he'd be so perfect for her."

They were on the plane together, coming back from Venice. Dinner had just been cleared away in the first-class section, and now Colleen, a blanket tucked around her, had her head snuggled on Charlie's shoulder as he read a copy of the *New York Times*.

"What about Thanksgiving?"

"Mmm?" Charlie gave up trying to read the paper and set it down in his lap. "Thanksgiving? Wasn't Pierre going to cook for us?"

"Yes, and Alex is coming, but I thought perhaps we could go to a polo game next week and perhaps see Sean, and maybe you could invite him to have Thanksgiving with us. I'll bet money that he'll come if he thinks he'll have a chance of seeing Alex."

"I didn't know I was married to such a schemer."

"Oh, darling." She snuggled closer to him as his arm came up around her shoulders. "You told me, a long time ago, that all's fair in love and war."

"So I did," he said, remembering, and he grinned.

"WELL, THE BACHELOR BASH went off without a hitch. And Muffy has had three bridal showers already," Phillip said to Rachel as they jogged along the gravel path that led up one of the hills. "So everything is going pretty much as we planned it."

"I thought the papers might be a good way for you to keep in touch with what's going on."

"I'm getting a little tired of hanging out here, though."

"Me, too. I'll be glad when the colonel opens the bidding and we can take off. It's the pits, stuck here for

Thanksgiving. The only good thing about it is that maybe I can talk someone else into making a turkey."

Phillip hugged his arms close to his lean, athletic body. His breath was coming out of his mouth in white puffs. "I cook a mean bird."

"Great. Then I can just do what I like to do—the pies and cranberry sauce."

"We'll make the best of it. But I can't wait to get home."

MARCY GLANCED UP as Louise walked by, humming softly.
How strange. Louise doesn't hum.

There were some things in life Marcy didn't quite understand. Like, for one, how Louise had managed to wangle a job as assistant caterer, while Marcy herself was still working as a personal assistant. She'd cleaned up enough of Louise's messes before she'd figured out that the woman was using her. Marcy was sure she could put together a wedding, bar mitzvah or an anniversary if the occasion arose.

But she still couldn't get up the nerve to tell Alex how she felt.

It was something she wanted so badly that the words froze in her throat. She'd tried to talk to Alex once, before she'd taken on the Bradford wedding, but had ended up talking about something else, then kicking herself all the way home.

It was her dream to be able to put weddings together the same way Alex did, with as much flair and style as her boss. Marcy grimaced, then picked up a pencil and began to doodle on the pad in front of her. Now, she spent all her time and frustration on her wardrobe, putting all her sense of style and design into what she wore into the office every day.

She knew Alex would listen to her. She knew she could do it. Why was she so afraid?

The phone rang. Marcy sighed and picked up the receiver.

THE CRYSTAL BALLROOM.

Alex walked silently through the immense ballroom, trying to visualize what it would look like once the wedding of the year was truly under way.

The room was magnificent. Bas-relief sculptures of Queen Isabella and Christopher Columbus enticed guests into a room that was defined by gilded Corinthian pillars and stunning half-moon balconies. From its domed ceiling hung two original crystal-laced chandeliers imported from Europe. They were immense, measuring almost twelve feet in diameter. The ceiling, covered with mythical figures painted by Giovanni Smeraldi, gave the room a truly European feel.

The rugs had been designed to complement the exquisite ceiling, and patterns of roses, reds and greens swirled beneath Alex's feet.

The whole effect was opulent, rich, elegant and simply beautiful. And in a way, Alex had to admit to herself as she slowly crossed the empty ballroom, Constance had been brilliant to insist on a Renaissance theme. The architectural decorations inside the Biltmore were reflective of the Spanish-Italian Renaissance.

Pierre and his staff were endlessly experimenting with various dishes, trying to inject a little California *nouvelle* into the Renaissance cuisine they were supposed to be copying.

The room would be transformed into a wonderland, a place so far removed from downtown Los Angeles that it would be hard to believe modern-day traffic, noise and congestion were merely yards away.

Alex's mind was full of the staggering details: one hundred and twenty-five thousand dollars' worth of flowers, a formal sit-down dinner for eight hundred people, hours of music and entertainment, jugglers and dancers and minstrels, and, of course, the several braces of pheasants.

Muffy, in her Belgian lace gown and long train. And Sean... She smiled as she remembered Constance's controlled look of fury when she had informed her that he was not going to wear a morning suit with tails, waistcoat, and top hat. He had opted instead for a very elegant tuxedo, tailored to his specifications. Very simple and reserved.

Sean's defiance of Constance had impressed Alex. He was most definitely his own man. The only member of the wedding that disturbed her was Muffy.

Pale and wan, the girl seemed to be growing sicker by the minute. Alex still hadn't seen Muffy and Sean together, but she'd believed Sean when he'd told her that this marriage involved loyalty, nothing more.

In her own mind, Alex had convinced herself that this was nothing more than a marriage of convenience, like in the romance novels she'd read. It had to be. Muffy was lifeless. Listless.

Sean was a passionate man.

The room was silent and she continued her solitary walk. *Oh, if these walls could talk . . .*

There were so many stories connected with the Biltmore. The hotel's colorful history and its gracious architecture, which made you feel you were stepping back in time to a gracious European royal estate, were the two reasons Alex loved working here. The building was like a living, breathing entity.

She stopped in the middle of the room and closed her eyes. Alex, deep inside, was a dreamer, and now she wondered what that first ball must have been like, when the hotel opened in the fall of 1923. There had been three thousand guests, and the Biltmore had been called the grandest hotel west of Chicago.

But it was a Los Angeles landmark, inextricably tied to the film industry. Oscar had been born in the Crystal Ballroom, when the Academy of Motion Picture Arts and Sciences held its first organizational banquet. The famous statuette had been created from some scribblings on a ta-

blecloth, and many Academy Awards dinners and presentations had been held at the Biltmore through 1941.

European royalty and American presidents had slept in
this hotel, the most recent visitors having been the Duke and
Duchess of York.

It was a world Alex loved, and she knew this wedding was
going to be the culmination of so many hard years of work,
a major event in her career.

The hotel, with her gentle, benevolent spirit, had also
brought Sean into Alex's life, and for that alone, she would
always be eternally grateful.

"Thank you," she whispered fancifully into the dark
room. "You're a real grande dame."

"YEAH, I'VE FIXED HER. Oh, no, nothing that simple. I'll
tell you over dinner. No, not Max's. Let's go to that new
place out on the pier."

Marcy froze, hearing the genuine malice in Louise's tone.
They were both working late, but she was sure Louise had
no idea Marcy could hear this conversation. She'd picked up
the wrong extension by mistake, and now didn't dare set
down the receiver for fear of being discovered inadvertently eavesdropping.

"Little Miss Rich Bitch thinks the rules just don't apply
to her," Louise continued in a low, satisfied voice. "Well, I
know exactly how to nail her to the wall. She's always on top
of me, nagging. She picks on me, Randy. I've told her some
of the ways I thought she could run this office more effec-
tively, but she just puts me down all the time. And in front
of the others. Nobody likes me here because of her attitude, and I've just had it. I don't deserve treatment like
this."

Marcy, her hand over the mouthpiece of her receiver,
grimaced. Alex, pick on Louise? It was the exact opposite.
Louise was one of those women who genuinely believed the
world owed her a living. She'd lived with a rich guy at the

beach for three years, and when he'd dumped her, he'd called Alex and asked her a friendly favor. Could she take Louise on and teach her the ropes so that the poor woman would have a salable skill?

Alex had bent over backward, and now Louise was going to stick it to her.

Not if I can help it.

"No, I don't want to talk about it over the phone." Marcy could hear Louise pause to take a long drag on one of the endless cigarettes she smoked over the course of a working day. "But let me tell you—" now there was a hint of laughter in her voice "—Constance Bradford is going to crucify her when my little bomb drops."

Marcy froze, barely breathing. When Louise finally hung up, she set the receiver down in its cradle and stared blindly in front of her.

The Bradford wedding. She's going to try to destroy Alex's career.

But how? And why? Louise's vindictiveness was all out of proportion to anything Alex could have done to her.

Louise would pass her desk on the way out. She'd see her. Possibly suspect she'd been overheard.

Grabbing her purse, Marcy slipped out the elegant, brass-trimmed glass doors and ran silently down the hall.

Chapter Eight

"Well, I'm just glad you and Uncle Charlie got home safely." Alex had been worried about her aunt and uncle flying to Europe. Any time she watched the news, it seemed someone was sabotaging some flight. Though she loved to travel and had gone on many memorable trips with Charlie and Colleen, there really was no place like home.

Colleen swam smoothly to the side of the pool, then grasped the steel ladder and climbed up to the smooth concrete.

"I'm glad you could come over for a morning swim. Are we still on for Thanksgiving?"

"I wouldn't miss it."

"Where are your parents going?"

"They'll be in New York. My father has some business he has to take care of."

"I wish James would slow down. He can't keep up this pace."

"Try telling him. Mother does all the time. Where's Charlie?"

"He's at the club."

"Why don't you two play golf together anymore?"

"Well," Colleen said, scratching Beluga behind his ears, "would you play golf with someone who cheats, lies and refuses to pay off when he loses?"

"No," Alex admitted truthfully.

"Well, neither will Charlie."

After she'd finished laughing, Alex looked ruefully at her aunt. "That joke is old!"

"I know, but it made you laugh, and that's what counts."

They ate out on the patio, fresh melon and eggs Benedict. Colleen had an excellent cook, who usually prepared diet dishes for Colleen and her husband. But when company came over, she liked to go all out.

"That hollandaise is as good as anything we prepare at the Biltmore," Alex admitted as she sat back in the white wrought-iron chair and stretched.

"You didn't eat too much of it."

"Nervous stomach, I guess."

"How are things going with that man of yours? Do you mind if I ask?"

Alex could see that her aunt was dying to know more, but she changed the subject. Even though she was growing more and more sure of Sean's feelings for her, it still sounded too strange to be put into words. She was under a lot of pressure at the moment, and she didn't need any more. Not that she thought her aunt would make her life more complicated, but she just wanted to keep things to herself a little longer.

"I understand." Colleen patted her hand. "When Charlie and I first found each other, I didn't want to talk about it, either. It was too special."

"Thank you, Colleen."

"Be happy, darling, it's all over much too quickly." She glanced at her watch as she picked it up from the glass-topped table and fastened it to her wrist. "And though you know I love having you here, you'd better get moving if you want to beat the traffic."

"MARCY? ALEX."

"What's up?"

"I don't know. I'm not feeling too well. Do you think you could try and cancel that four o'clock with Mrs. Weaver? Then I could leave before three."

"It's as good as done."

Hanging up the phone, Alex cradled her head in her hands and stared dully at her desk. All those late nights and careless meals had caught up with her. There was a strain of the flu going around the office, and she was just about sure she was in the early stages.

Not one who believed in working while she was sick and spreading disease throughout the catering offices, she left the office promptly at three and drove straight home. She fed Roscoe so he'd leave her alone, then crawled into bed and decided to sweat it out.

THE PHONE RANG, and Marcy automatically picked it up.

"Catering offices, can I help you?"

"Is Alex there?"

"She's sick, Sean. She went home at three."

"What's wrong? Is it serious?"

"Just a case of the current crud going around the office. She'll probably be back in a few days."

There was a slight hesitation over the line, and Marcy said softly, "I bet you'd like her home address, right?"

"You got it."

"Your brother better be cute."

"I think you'll like him."

"Got a pencil ready?"

HE WAS AT Alex's house in record time, with takeout chicken soup from a deli, a fresh loaf of bread and everything he could think of from the pharmacy that might make things more comfortable for her.

But he hadn't counted on a blond bombshell in nothing more than a long pink paint-stained cotton T-shirt opening the door.

"Does Alex live here?"

"The other side of the house. I'm Karin."

"Sean."

The brilliant blue eyes narrowed in the lightly tanned face. "Aren't you the guy who's marrying Muffy Bradford?"

"One and the same."

"And you're bringing Alex chicken soup in bed— Forget it, it's none of my business. But mess around with my buddy's head, and I'll break both your legs."

He couldn't suppress a smile. "I'll take that into consideration."

"Good. Just so you know." She smiled, then closed the door.

He walked around to the other door and knocked, but there was no answer.

"I've got a spare key if you want it."

He glanced around to find Karin behind him, now in a pair of well-worn jeans as well as the pink shirt.

He couldn't resist asking the obvious. "Why would you help me out?"

"I guess," she said slowly, her face breaking into a mischievous grin, "because I really do believe in blowing out your valves once in a while."

"I beg your pardon?"

"Ask Alex."

HE HEATED UP THE SOUP, moving quietly through the kitchen so as not to wake her. The house was exactly as he had imagined it would be, large and airy with white walls, framed prints, two overstuffed striped sofas, modern furniture, polished wooden floors and a healthy collection of books and magazines piled along the stairway and in several huge bookcases.

Alex had made herself a home.

But it looked as though she didn't spend much time there. Her refrigerator had been depressingly empty, and there was just the slightest bit of dust in the living room.

The Bradford wedding was escalating, taking up more and more of her time.

When the soup boiled, he made some toast, then put together a tray and started upstairs.

He knocked gently on the one closed door upstairs, and when no one answered, opened it and stepped inside.

ALEX HAD BEEN DREAMING, strange, unpleasant dreams, as she tossed and turned in bed, trying to get comfortable.

When she saw Sean come in the door of her bedroom, she thought she had to be hallucinating.

"What are you doing here?"

"I've come to take care of you. Marcy told me you weren't feeling well."

Alex, as sick as she was, still automatically reached to the far side of the bed and slid the stack of books beneath the dust ruffle.

Some things were still better left a mystery.

"What's that?"

"Chicken soup and toast. Nature's perfect food."

She managed a weak smile. "I was going to make myself something to eat later on, but I guess I could eat now."

"Do you feel like eating?"

"I'm not nauseous. I just feel horrible."

"Stressed out. I'm not surprised. Why don't you try to eat a little, and then I'll give you an alcohol rub."

Alex knew she was ill when not a single sensual thought flashed into her brain.

After the back rub, he carried her downstairs and, wrapped in a blanket and deep in the cushions of one of the sofas, Alex had to admit she felt a lot better.

"Why do you resist being taken care of?" Sean asked. They had been watching game shows for the past hour, and now they were both trying to complete a crossword puzzle. Alex was doing a lot more light dozing than actually concentrating on the puzzle.

"I do not."

"You certainly do."

"I—wasn't aware of it."

"It gives me great pleasure to look after you. Is that all right with you, Alex?"

Tears stung her eyes as she closed them, resting her head against one of the pillows Sean had brought downstairs. For as long as she could remember, she had felt something of a stranger in her parents' home, only feeling comfortable when she was with her aunt and uncle. But even though she had transferred so much of her affection to Colleen and Charlie, they still didn't fill the void her parents had left inside her.

She had always wondered, from a very small age, why they had even bothered to have a child.

"I'm sorry," she whispered.

"No, no, I didn't mean it like that," Sean said, his voice gentle. "It's just that, how are you going to get better if you don't let me take care of you, just a little?"

"Okay. I think I would like that."

"HELLO, MARCY, could I speak to Alex, please?"

"She's not here, Colleen. She didn't feel well, and she went home."

"Oh. I thought she looked a little funny this morning. Maybe I'll take a drive out there and see if she needs anything. Thank you, Marcy."

"But—Sean's already there," Marcy said slowly, speaking to a buzzing phone. She hung up slowly, then shrugged her shoulders and returned her attention to a list she had compiled.

It was a master list of everything being done for the Bradford wedding. If Louise was trying to deliberately sabotage the wedding, she had to have contacted someone who was providing a major service. Marcy had already called Pierre and double-checked with him. All the food preparations were coming along nicely. The next thing she'd done was call the costume agency and reconfirm the order on almost a hundred costumes.

Now, looking at the long list in front of her, she wished she had the nerve to throttle Louise and stick burning bamboo shoots beneath those perfectly manicured nails.

But that would let her know she was on to her destructive little game.

No, she'd have to do things this way, even if it took more time away from what she was supposed to be doing.

Sighing, Marcy picked up the phone.

SEAN WAS SITTING on the sofa opposite Alex, watching her sleep, when he heard the bell ring.

When he answered the back door, the woman stepped briskly inside, an enormous black Chow Chow right behind her.

"I'm Alex's aunt, Colleen Michaels. And you are—"

"Sean. Sean Lawton. I'm . . . a friend of your niece's."

He knew she'd noticed the slight hesitation, but she'd smiled.

"How is she?"

"Sleeping. She ate some soup and toast, then I moved her downstairs, and we've been watching television. I think it's just exhaustion."

"I would say so. I think my niece has had a lot on her mind."

There was nothing in the statement that was a condemnation, yet Sean had the strangest feeling she knew exactly what was going on.

"Oh, this is Beluga. He's harmless, unless you're standing in the way of his supper dish. I think I'll stay a bit, have a cup of coffee and see if she wakes up."

"I've already got coffee made."

"How resourceful. I like that in a man."

They sat in the kitchen, drinking coffee and talking. Somewhere along the line, Sean pulled out the small box of cookies he'd picked up at the deli along with the soup, and Beluga became his friend for life over a chocolate-dipped butter cookie.

They were in the middle of their fourth cup apiece when the phone rang. Sean answered it on the first thing, not wanting Alex to wake up.

"Sean? Marcy. I have some paperwork Alex will want to see, so I'm going to drop it by on my way home. Will you be there?"

"Yes. I'm not going to leave her alone."

He missed the small, satisfied smile that curved Colleen's lips.

"I need to talk to you about something."

"Yes, Brian is coming to the wedding."

"No, this is something I need help with. And I don't want Alex to know about it until she absolutely has to."

The serious tone in her voice disturbed him. "Of course. I'll be here, and I'll do whatever I can."

Back at the table, he picked up his coffee and contemplated it, worried.

"Something upsetting?"

"Something's not right at the office. Marcy's dropping some paperwork by, but this has nothing to do with any paperwork. It's just an excuse to come over."

"Perhaps something to do with your wedding?"

Now he could sense her studying his face, watching for the slightest change of expression.

"It wouldn't surprise me." He kept his voice perfectly flat and unemotional, then changed the subject.

Twenty minutes later, Colleen rose, took her coffee cup to the sink and rinsed it out, then snapped her fingers. Beluga, who had been lying at Sean's feet and staring up at him worshipfully—all the time hoping for another butter cookie—stood up, stretched, then began to wag his tightly curled tail.

"I don't think she's going to wake up soon. The best thing is for her to get as much sleep as possible. And, as I feel she's in very good hands, I'll leave her with you."

Sean got up out of his chair and walked her to the back door.

Colleen didn't mince words. "I hope that whatever happens, Sean, you won't end up hurting her."

"That was never my intention."

"I'm not quite sure if I understand what's going on here. However, I've loved my niece from the first day I caught sight of her at the hospital, and I've done everything in my power to keep her from harm. Alex is very special to me."

"I understand."

"And, though it is totally beyond my comprehension at this point in time, I'm getting very good feelings about the two of you."

"Thank you."

"What are you doing for Thanksgiving?"

He thought of the probable dinner at the Bradfords', and having to sit across from Constance for another interminable evening.

"I haven't made any plans yet."

"You're welcome at our house, if you'd like to spend the day with Alex."

He smiled. "Am I that transparent? I'd love to."

"You can get my address from Alex. Come on, Beluga."

He watched her as she walked to the car, the fluffy black dog trotting directly beside her and to the left. For as much of a mooch as Beluga was, Colleen had trained him well.

You don't have to worry, Colleen. I can't see myself getting far, what with Pierre's poisoned wedding cake and two broken legs.

He poured himself another cup of coffee and waited for Marcy.

"SO I DON'T KNOW where she's messed things up, but something's going to go wrong. I've called almost halfway down this master list, and everything is still on schedule. It gets me crazy. If I hadn't picked up the wrong extension that night, no one would know about this."

"Why aren't you doing Louise's job instead of Louise? You're a lot more competent than she is."

Sean knew he'd hit a nerve when Marcy dropped her gaze to the table and whispered, "I don't know."

"Have you talked to Alex?"

"No, I haven't. I guess I'm just a real chicken. I've tried a couple of times, but the words just stick in my throat." She played nervously with the cashmere scarf tied at her throat. The Aviatrix look, complete with a soft suede bomber jacket over a leather flying suit and designer boots, was a natural on Marcy's slim figure.

"You can't go anywhere in life if you don't even know where you want to go."

"Yeah, but what if I can't do it?"

"What's the worst that can happen? Could you do as bad a job as Louise has?"

"*No one* could do as bad a job as she does."

"Why is it you feel you can't make any mistakes? I've made some real beauties, and I'm still around."

"You? Come on, you're Mr. Successful."

"Not all the time."

"Really?"

"Think about a baby learning to walk. You get up, you misjudge, you fall down. You grab the edge of a table, haul yourself up again, keep going, overestimate and fall down. But a baby doesn't sit in the middle of a room and think, 'Well, I fell down twice, I'd better not try this anymore.'

They keep going until they work it out and get it right. It's the same thing with any job.''

"I never looked at it like that. So I never give myself a chance to see if I can do it—"

"Then you're just sitting in the middle of the floor. And that's no way to live.''

"You're right. So the first thing I have to do is ask Alex.''

"Right.''

"Ask Alex what?''

Sean turned toward the sound of her voice. Alex was leaning in the doorway, wrapped tightly in a turquoise-and-purple paisley silk robe with silk tassels. Her long hair was loose and in a gentle tangle to her waist. She looked much better, her face less exhausted, her eyes clearer.

Sean stood up and helped her into one of the kitchen chairs, then touched her forehead gently.

"Not as hot as before. Do you want some juice? I brought orange and apple.''

"Apple, please.'' But Alex was not to be deterred. "Ask me what?''

Marcy stole a quick, beseeching glance at Sean. He shook his head.

"It's in your corner, kiddo.''

Marcy cleared her throat. Her hands grasped the edge of the table tightly, then she said, rushing the words out at breakneck speed. "Alex, it's just that I've always wanted a chance to see if I could do some catering work. And I know I could! I've watched you and Phil and Lisa, even Louise. I couldn't be as bad as she is. So, do you think I might be able to—you know, have a chance to do something?''

Alex's expression was clearly incredulous, and Sean almost laughed out loud.

"You never said a word about wanting to cater, Marcy.''

The redhead's hands were relaxing, her fingers unclenching as she let go of the table edge. "I just didn't think I could do it.''

"Why not? Don't you think I know exactly who was responsible for the Higgins wedding last spring? It wasn't Louise."

"You knew? I really felt stupid about that one. She used me until I got smart and stopped doing her work for her."

"Well," said Sean, setting a glass of apple juice down in front of Alex, "you can take over Louise's job once she's fired."

Alex sighed. "I can't fire Louise. There's too much work."

"Give Marcy the job. Louise isn't doing her work, anyway. And she's actively trying to destroy your own."

Alex's dark gaze was steady as she spoke. "What are you talking about?"

Sean glanced at Marcy, sure that he was doing the right thing. "She has to know. Alex may be able to figure out just what it is Louise is up to."

Quickly, Marcy filled Alex in on the conversation she'd overheard, then explained about the list she'd made up and the checking she'd been doing.

"She's thrown a wrench into the works somewhere, but I can't seem to find it."

"Give me the list," Alex said quietly.

They were all silent as she scanned the list a first time, then a second. On the third time through, she found what she was looking for.

"The flowers."

"How do you know?" Sean said, admiration in his voice. He respected people who used their instincts, and Alex's were working overtime.

"I'm sure it's the flowers. Constance Bradford could forgive everything else, but she wants flowers that will outshine the Jamison wedding, she was quite clear about that. And if you botch a flower order, it's not like Pierre can whip up something else in his kitchen to cover your butt. You can't get flowers that are *that* special anywhere else but David's.''

"How could she have screwed up the order?" Marcy asked.

"It's my guess that David's pretty furious with me right now. All Louise had to do was call him up and cancel the order, implying that his flowers weren't good enough and we were going to use someone else. He's good—I think he's the best—but he's temperamental, and he doesn't always check things through. And he's the perfect choice because he'd be too proud to call me and scream at me. He'd just never do business with me again.''

"So what are we going to do?" Marcy asked.

"Tomorrow morning, early, the three of us will go to his store. This will be a nice little piece of on-the-job training for you, Marcy.''

"And if the flowers have been cancelled?" Sean asked.

"Louise's history.''

THE ELEVATOR DOOR slid open and Alex stepped out, then walked swiftly down the hallway toward the catering offices. She knew Marcy was already at her desk, as her personal-assistant-soon-to-be-assistant-caterer had gone on ahead of her.

She pushed open the brass-trimmed glass doors and spoke quietly to Marcy.

"Send Louise in.''

Her stomach was in knots. This was possibly the worst part of being the director of catering, but it had to be done. And her lingering fury gave her the strength she was going to need to face the scene ahead.

David Russell had been furious with her. The one hundred and twenty-five thousand dollar flower order had been cancelled, and implications had been made that his flower arrangements for the Jamison wedding had been "not quite good enough" for the Bradfords. When Alex had swept into his store that morning, she'd barely closed the door behind her when he'd started screaming.

After his outburst, she hadn't minced words. She'd told him exactly what happened, then soothed his artist's ego and made sure the flowers were reordered.

Now Louise was going to get exactly what she deserved.

It was unfortunate, but Alex had learned that men and women tended to do things very differently. Men, while they had problems in other areas, were generally direct when they needed to confront you. If an idea was stolen on the floor, you could count on the affronted man coming to the person who had wronged him and directly confronting him.

Women were a different story. Alex found that her female co-workers tended to try all sorts of petty little things in order to "get back" at who had wronged them. They rarely confronted problems directly and tended to go behind the person's back.

Learning to deal with problems directly and training herself to be able to confront was the hardest thing Alex had ever had to learn. It went against everything she had been taught to do. You could not possibly be the classic "good girl" and make it anywhere in upper management.

What Louise had done was not a simple matter of hiding a box of pencils or destroying a telling memo. It wasn't even in league with hiding necessary paperwork and having it "turn up" a day too late in order to make someone look mildly incompetent.

This woman was out for blood. And her actions were going to have devastating consequences.

"Hi, Alex, you wanted something?"

"Louise. Sit down." Alex's tone was pleasant, as if nothing was wrong.

Louise sat, and Alex gave her a long, steady, assessing look.

The woman was incredible. She didn't even flinch.

"Louise, I think it's in both of our best interests to get straight to the point."

The expression in Louise's round blue eyes was just the tiniest bit nervous.

"I spoke with David Russell today, and it seems that the order for the Bradford flowers was cancelled. Do you know anything about it?"

Blue eyes opened even wider, but Alex didn't miss the slight trembling of her hands.

"No. Should I?"

With those three words, Louise sealed her fate. Alex would have respected her more if she had told the truth.

"I know you did, Louise. Clear out your desk and be out of here within the hour. Don't ever ask me for a reference. I don't think I could stomach it."

The blue eyes narrowed. "You think you're such a—"

Marcy, with perfect timing, opened the door to Alex's office. "Alex, Sean is here to see you. Are you busy with anything?"

"Nothing of any real consequence," she said, looking straight at Louise. "I don't want to see you again before you leave."

Louise opened her mouth, seemed to think better of it, then turned and walked swiftly out of the office. She barely spared Sean a glance as they met in the doorway.

"So, you told her?"

"She lied. I didn't expect her to admit it."

"Well, I thought you might be in need of a little rescuing. Pierre is bringing up some food for you to taste, and as I know your next appointment isn't until ten-thirty, I thought I'd join you."

Alex smiled, and took the hand he held out to her, then let him pull her into his arms.

"She was pretty nasty."

"I would have expected her to be."

"But I'm glad she's gone." She looked up into his face. "And I'm glad you're here."

TIME PASSED WITH amazing swiftness as the Bradford wedding drew closer and closer. The days grew shorter, and Alex's evenings grew longer as her workload continued to increase. She didn't want to look too far into the future, didn't want to think about the wedding of the year and what was going to happen afterward.

She simply immersed herself in her work and enjoyed the time she had with Sean.

She packed all her self-help books in several cardboard boxes and donated them to the library.

She stopped making lists, as there was no point to it. A list couldn't help her see where her life was going.

And slowly, ever so slowly, Alex began to believe that events were unfolding the way they were for a reason, and she gave up trying to control her life.

It was so much more fun just living it.

Chapter Nine

There were still times when Alex thought the entire arrangement was less than perfect. She wondered what was actually going to happen on the day the Bradford wedding took place. Sean didn't seem the sort of man who could marry one woman and keep another one as his cookie on the side.

There were even a few times when she went out to parties on her own, particularly nights when Sean had to work late. In a way, these evenings were therapeutic, as the men she met there reinforced the fact that Sean wasn't anything like them.

"Catering! Wow, like, you could make cupcakes then, right?"

"The Biltmore? That's that ship down in Long Beach, isn't it? What's it like to work on a boat?"

"Oh, you're one of those hard-bitten career types. But you'd give it all up if the right man came along, wouldn't you?"

And the perennial favorite: "What's your sign?"

After these bouts with the general public, Alex would slink home, take a hot shower, put on her favorite robe, sometimes light a fire and pour herself a glass of wine, then stare into the flames—or run upstairs, jump into bed and pull the quilt over her head—and wonder how it was possible that a man as wonderful as Sean had simply dropped into her life.

She didn't want to lose him. But she couldn't see herself living with some kind of "arrangement" with a married man. She felt guilty enough spending the time she did with Sean while he was engaged to another woman. Since the night he'd kidnapped her in Marcy's fur coat and taken her up to his suite, she hadn't spent any nights in his bed. They talked on the phone a lot. He stopped by her office on the pretext of seeing how the wedding was coming along. They shared lunches in the privacy of Pierre's kitchen. She'd even invited him over to her house for dinner twice—take-out Chinese one night, steaks and salad the other.

He left promptly at ten-thirty both evenings, and Alex hadn't been sure whether to be touched or depressed that he hadn't made any kind of pass. There were times when she thought she had hallucinated that entire kiss in her office, but she had only to close her eyes to find it had been indelibly burned into her memory.

Now it was simply a matter of time. The Bradford wedding was set for December 20, and Thanksgiving was just two days away. She knew Sean was going to be a guest at Charlie and Colleen's annual dinner, and she was looking forward to it. There was so much to do as the wedding drew closer and closer that on many days she didn't have the time to dwell on her predicament for more than a few minutes at a time.

Yet the knowledge was always there, like a softly ticking bomb ready to explode or be defused.

She and Sean were upstairs in his penthouse, eating dinner, when she brought up some of the thoughts that had been troubling her.

"Sean," she said slowly, twirling the tines of her fork through the pasta with scallops, shrimp and a light basil-and-tomato sauce, "I keep wondering what's going to happen on the day of the wedding. I know I promised to trust you and to believe that everything is going to work out, but I keep having all these doubts.''

He set down his wineglass and looked at her, his gaze open and direct. ''I'll be able to tell you everything three days before the wedding. You won't have to go through the ceremony wondering how everything is going to work out. But I can't until then, Alex. There are other people involved whose futures depend on my discretion. And I think a certain amount of knowledge too far in advance might make things difficult for you when you work with Constance.''

Alex sighed, then picked up her wineglass. What Sean said made sense. Constance Bradford was in and out of her office or consulting with her on the phone almost every day. And talking with the woman only depressed Alex.

At the beginning of the Bradford wedding plans, it had almost been possible to believe that Constance had some genuine feeling for her daughter and was truly trying to give her the wedding of the year, a day she and her groom would remember for the rest of their lives. But as Alex got to know the woman, it became more and more clear that Constance was in her glory planning this society bash, the premier A-list holiday party of December, and that it had nothing at all to do with her daughter's happiness.

Alex had said as much to Sean one evening and would never forget his tone of voice or the look in his eyes when he'd answered her.

''Women and money can be a deadly mix.''

Now, thinking about that reply, she realized that there was so much she didn't know about this man, so much she wanted to find out.

''Have you gone out with a lot of women who were only interested in your money?'' she asked softly, setting her fork down and leaning back in her chair.

''To be perfectly honest, before I met you, I didn't know there was any other kind of woman on earth.''

Comprehension dawned, and with it came sudden understanding. "That was why you had me investigated."

Sean still had the grace to look slightly uncomfortable about that move. "Alex, you made me feel totally out of control, and I'm still not sure I like the feeling."

"Join the club."

He smiled and took another sip of wine. "The only thing on my mind when I went ahead and had an investigator friend of mine put together a file on you was that I didn't want to feel as passionately about you as I did if all you were interested in was my bank account. But you were so different from what I'd come to expect. You made your own money. You'd walked away from your father's. I knew then, from reading the report, that you were a woman with a very distinct set of values."

It was the question of values that stumped her. She was sure, her newly trusted instincts were just screaming that Sean was a man who could be trusted, not some disreputable womanizer. Unlike most of the men she had met before and during her sabbatical from the opposite sex, he had a very clear idea of what was right and wrong for him. She'd picked up the slightest bit of discomfort whenever he'd talked about the impending wedding. He didn't even like to talk about it all that much, changing the subject gracefully and going on to other things.

He was very careful concerning what he said about Muffy, keeping their relationship absolutely private, and this trait, far from frustrating Alex, made Sean all the more endearing. There was something so terribly protective in his relationship with Muffy.

She believed him when he said he didn't love Muffy. She believed him when he'd told her he loved her.

She just couldn't figure out what was going to happen on December 20, and it was driving her crazy.

Many evenings, Alex drove home around nine or ten, with just enough time to take a hot bath, make herself a cup of tea and tuck herself into bed. Then, when she found herself too wound up to sleep, she'd reach for a cookbook, now that all her self-help books were at the library helping someone else.

Karin had taken one look at her frazzled state and recommended a new book she had just bought, with recipes for comfort food. So Alex immersed herself in fat roast chicken with buttery bread stuffing, French toast nursery-style, fritters and fried tomatoes with cream sauce. She read on, delving a little deeper into the large book each night. Molasses cookies, mashed potatoes and mile-high apple pie. Strawberry shortcake, spoon bread and scalloped tomatoes.

She didn't even miss Roscoe biting her toes. On one of the evenings Sean had been over for dinner, she had confessed her dislike for the tabby tom cat, and Sean had offered to take him off her hands. Quicker than she could say "but he doesn't really like strangers," Roscoe had been in Sean's arms, purring and looking utterly content. Sean hadn't even needed a carrier, he'd simply carried Roscoe to his car, locked both of them in and headed off to the Biltmore.

It was sheer luxury knowing that you could sleep soundly at night without getting your toes bitten off. And Alex replaced the batteries in her smoke alarm—just in case.

She found herself in a holding pattern, and even though there were moments when she felt extreme anxiety, she could not remember a time she had looked forward to the holidays with more delight.

"You really miss her, don't you?" Rachel's voice was concerned.

"I just wish I could talk to Muffy. That picture I saw of her in the paper looked terrible. She was holding on to Sean's arm as if she'd collapse without his support."

They were in the kitchen of the Virginia farmhouse. Rachel was making cranberry sauce, then she was going to start on the pumpkin pies. Phillip was restlessly chain-smoking and contemplating opening another bottle of Scotch.

"You'll be out of here soon enough. The holidays are always stressful. Does Muffy know when to expect you?"

"I told her I would figure out a way to contact her when I got to Los Angeles. Just to let her know I was in town and everything was going as planned. I don't know. I just feel so damn helpless, sitting here and doing nothing."

"What could you do now, if you were in L.A.?"

Phillip considered this question for a moment, then said quietly, "Nothing. If anything, I think things are going smoother without me there, because that—Constance has no reason to be suspicious."

"There. You see?" Rachel searched through the spice rack until she found the cinnamon sticks and added one to the pot of cranberries, sugar and water. "You'd be doing both you and Muffy more harm than good even if you were out there."

She stirred the bubbling cranberry sauce, then glanced at the clock on the farmhouse kitchen wall. "You can only lend her your support, but you can't do it for her. She wouldn't appreciate it if you did."

"I know. I know."

"Besides, you told me that Sean always has everything perfectly under control."

"He does." Phillip sighed as Rachel turned off the gas burner and transferred the saucepan to another, cooler burner, still stirring. "He told me once that he had never been in love, and that as far as he was concerned it was more trouble than it was worth. For the first time in my life, I'm beginning to see the wisdom of his way of thinking."

"Oh, give me a break," Rachel said, getting out the canned pumpkin, half-and-half and eggs she'd need to make the pies. "You men. Invulnerable. All-powerful. Let me let you in on a little secret. The bigger they are, the harder they fall."

"No, not Sean. Control is his middle name."

SEAN LAWTON HAD never felt more out of control in his entire life. He lay in bed, Roscoe on his chest, and stared at the ceiling.

Alexandra. The look in her soft brown eyes when she tried to ask him a question that might put both her heart and mind at ease. The way she looked at him when she thought he couldn't see her. The slightest of hesitations when they were together, as if she could still prevent what was happening between them. As if there were the slightest possibility they could distance themselves from each other.

Never.

He hated not being able to tell her. But he couldn't break a confidence. Phillip and Muffy were counting on him, and he was beginning to worry whether Muffy was going to be up for this.

Strangely enough, John Bradford seemed to sense that something was wrong with his daughter, with this entire affair. The few times they had talked, John had expressed concern. He had confided in him, had told him of Muffy's broken engagement to Phillip and had wondered if his daughter was ready for marriage.

Constance had fooled her husband, making it sound as though Phillip had used Muffy, then dumped her. And Sean had seen things for what they were quite clearly. Constance still had John fooled, with her classic Grace Kelly beauty and colder-than-ice persona. The benevolent dictator. She ran the Bradford household with military precision, hounded her daughter relentlessly, made it her mission in life to outdo, outshine, outspend anyone else in her social strata.

Constance was dedicated to keeping up with the Joneses—with a vengeance. Sean, the perfect son-in-law, merely fit in with the intricate master plan she had for herself. Not for Muffy.

Muffy. Something wasn't right. She was losing weight, her skin had a blue-veined transparency that almost frightened him. Her eyes often looked vacant, her smiles, infrequent as they were, were strained and overbright.

She needed Phillip, and he wouldn't be in Los Angeles until the evening of the seventeenth. It had been crazy to take the contract with Stealthco this close to the wedding, but in a way it had been a blessing.

Constance had an eagle eye when it came to her daughter, and Sean knew that Phillip and Muffy wouldn't have been able to keep away from each other. Someone would have slipped, and Constance would have done anything she had to to prevent her daughter from marrying a man with no financial future.

The perfect son-in-law, according to Constance, was incredibly rich, stupid and spineless enough to be led around by a ring in his nose. Sean had been aware that he fit the bill as far as the incredibly rich part went, but Constance knew she couldn't bully him. God knows she'd tried.

John Bradford, married to a woman like that, should have let her know in no uncertain terms that he was the master of his household. Instead, by being kind, he had called up nothing but his wife's contempt. With a certain kind of woman, being kind was an impossibility. Constance needed more than a firm hand. She needed to be put in her place with determined regularity. And if John Bradford had done that, she probably would have made his life a living hell until she found a man she could totally dominate.

She was an impossible woman. Serene on the surface, ugly underneath.

Sean took a deep breath, then slowly let it out, trying to relax. He scratched Roscoe's ears absently.

Would Alex forgive him when she found out the reason for his silence? Not an hour went by that he didn't think about the repercussions of what he was doing. He couldn't bear to think of losing her, the pain would be overwhelming. He hadn't realized how empty his life was until she had slipped into it.

Over the years, he'd thought he could continue on alone. Filling his life with friends and acquaintances, not ever needing anyone. But he needed Alex. Just walking into a room at the hotel and seeing her there made all the difference in the world in his day. Hearing her laugh. Arguing with her. Seeing her smile.

She'd touched his emotions in a way they had never been touched before, and now the thought of losing her was always uppermost in his mind.

It frightened him. And he wasn't a man who frightened easily.

When room service knocked, Roscoe shot off his chest and bolted for the door. Sean laughed, his humor restored. Roscoe made himself such a pest at mealtime that it had been necessary to order him mini cat meals, like a plate of flaked salmon without the salad or dressing. Now the cat was his devoted slave—or as much of a slave as a cat could ever be.

There was nothing Sean could do but wait. And pray that this entire scheme didn't blow up in his face.

"WONDERFUL TURKEY, Pierre."

"You outdid yourself with the stuffing."

"Ah, wait until you see what I have for dessert!"

There were unanimous groans around the table when Pierre presented three different desserts: a pumpkin chiffon pie, a killer pecan pie and a white-chocolate mousse in a pool of raspberry sauce.

Even Beluga was humbled.

Later, after everyone had eaten much more than they needed to and the cook had put away the food and cleaned up the kitchen, Charlie lit a fire in the large den and broke out a bottle of brandy.

"And what shall we drink to?" Colleen said from the depths of a black leather chair, Beluga lounging by her side.

"To love," Charlie said simply, his blue eyes twinkling. "To the many happy years we've had together, darling, and to many more."

"And to friends and family," Pierre added.

"And good food," Alex chimed in, raising her glass and looking at Pierre. She had her back to Sean and didn't dare look at him. She wanted to toast to love, but doubts were beginning to assail her again. Sean had fit in so perfectly with her aunt and uncle and Pierre, becoming part of the charmed circle of people she loved best in the world. She almost felt as if she couldn't get her hopes up too much, for fear of being hurt.

"And love," Sean said, his eyes on Alex's gleaming mane of hair, burnished by the firelight.

"And love," Charlie said, his sharp eyes taking it all in.

LATER, WHILE ALEX TOOK a short walk with Colleen and Beluga, and Pierre began to pack up his cooking equipment, Sean found himself alone in the den with Charlie.

The brandy had mellowed Sean, the fire was relaxing, and he found himself thinking that he hadn't enjoyed a Thanksgiving more in a long time.

But he was also smart enough to know Charlie wasn't going to waste an opportunity like this one.

"I think," Charlie said quietly, "that we'd better talk about Alex."

Sean said nothing. He respected this man's right to question him, taking on a father's role in wanting what was best for his niece.

"All right."

"You love her, but you're going to marry Muffy Bradford on the twentieth of December."

"Yes."

"What do you plan on doing about your relationship with my niece?"

"I'm not going to hurt her, Charlie."

"You're hurting her now," Charlie said quietly. "You're hurting her every time she looks at you and thinks she has absolutely no future with you. Are you scared of backing out of the wedding at this point?"

"No, sir, that's not it at all."

"I want you to know that if I had merely heard of what was going on, I would have never invited you here today. But Alexandra has such a high regard for you, and Colleen claims she's trusting her instincts where you're concerned. They're impeccable, and I've often trusted them myself. I just don't want to see my niece hurt badly."

"I understand."

"I doubt that you do. I think you need to know a little bit more about Alex than you do, and I don't think she's told you. So I'm taking it upon myself to trust you and fill you in on some of the details. Would you care to listen?"

Sean nodded his head.

"I'm about as different from my brother James as two people can be. I married Colleen because I fell in love with her. I still love her. James married Meredith because it was time to get married. He needed a wife. He went out looking for a woman to fill the role and came back with Meredith."

Sean said nothing, merely listened.

"Alexandra was born less than a year after their marriage. Meredith had a relatively easy birth, but children had not been part of what James saw in his future. He saw Meredith as his, a possession, an ornamentation. She was the woman who would accompany him on business trips, who would attend parties with him, who would entertain beautifully and ease his way up the ladder of success. There was no room for a child in that scenario.

"Apparently they hadn't talked about children. I have no doubts that Meredith wanted Alex, but she was a young girl, and James was—and is—an extremely persuasive man. He talked her into leaving Alex with Colleen and me when the child was six weeks old so she could accompany him to London on business."

Sean leaned forward ever so slightly.

"I accepted this arrangement, because Colleen and I had wanted children, but we weren't having any success. And, to be perfectly honest, Colleen had suffered through two miscarriages and a stillbirth, and I saw the look on her face when she first saw Alex at the hospital. My wife is an extremely giving woman, and I thought this time with Alex would be beneficial to her. I thought it would give her a chance to heal. She had so much love to give and nowhere for it to go.

"And Alex was an easy baby to love. The problem was, James's business trips became more frequent. Meredith began to realize she was being put in an untenable position, that of having to choose between her husband and her daughter. As I said, she was very young. A very frightened little thing. She chose James."

"What happened to Alex?"

"We raised her. But it was a painful childhood, knowing her father and mother were in the same city and had so little time for her. Colleen and I did the best we could, but it's not the same as your mother and father. No one ever takes their place in your heart, after all. No matter how bad they are at taking care of a family."

"I see."

"I hope you do. Alex rarely sees her father. The choices he made when she was a child were part of what was behind her decision to make it on her own. Meredith has tried, over the years, to build some kind of relationship with her daughter. And though Alex has been kind to her, I don't think she's ever truly forgiven her. It hasn't been easy for either of them.

"Colleen and I tried to give her all the love and support we could, but we decided not to lie about what happened. There was no way to soften it. As Alex grew older, my brother started to have affairs with various women. Meredith had nothing at this point, except the security that James would never divorce her. But a love affair for her was something he would have seen as grounds for cutting her out of his life entirely.

"She tried to bring Alex back into her life and only succeeded in confusing her. She wanted her, but then she sent her away. And I think Alex grew up with a sense of having done something terribly wrong and of never having been good enough."

Now Sean suddenly felt his throat tightening up, as he was sure he knew what Charlie was about to say.

"I don't ever," Charlie said quietly, "want anyone else to give her that feeling of not being good enough."

"MUFFY'S NOT feeling well. Bridal nerves, I suspect."

"I'd be nervous, too, if I was marrying Sean Lawton."

There were polite female titters around the table. Constance had invited over thirty people for a quiet little sit-down dinner, but she was displeased by her daughter's behavior. Muffy had come down with the flu and was upstairs in her bedroom, lying pale and wan in her bed. Constance, who would have preferred to have shown her daughter off, was highly displeased.

John Bradford, down at the other end of the long dining-room table, was studying his wife. Something wasn't right.

Muffy had always been a rather distant child toward him. Like most fathers of his generation, he had left the primary infant care to Constance and a battalion of nannies during the early years.

By the time Muffy was four years old, John hardly recognized the pale little girl as a child he could have fathered.

He had tried to be a father to her, but Muffy had seemed scared of him. And Constance had zealously guarded her time with her daughter, filling up the days with activities designed to sculpt Muffy into the perfect child.

He had been content with the leftovers. Until now.

Something had touched John Bradford deeply the day he had inadvertently walked in on his only daughter, lying in bed and sobbing as if her heart would break. He had tried to get her to tell him the specifics, but she had shaken her head, her entire manner one of the most abject despair.

Later that night, he had talked to Constance and learned that Phillip had used his daughter in the cruelest of fashions, then dumped her for another woman. It had made his blood boil with rage, and then he'd felt a sense of helplessness so complete it had made him feel older and more tired than he had in years.

He had made all the money a man could ever want, but he hadn't been able to spare his daughter from heartbreak.

Now, there was something that didn't quite feel right about this engagement and wedding. Sean and Muffy. The first time he'd seen them together, he'd thought they looked like a protective older brother with his delicate little sister. Perhaps that was what Muffy wanted—someone to protect her, watch over her. He had felt old and tired that day, as well, realizing he'd abdicated the role of father in so many ways.

Maybe it was just too late.

He glanced up, watching Constance at the other end of the long dining-room table. The chandelier gleamed softly above, the wallpaper was rich and opulent, a soft peach color. Silver clinked against china, and the crystal sparkled.

Everything was perfect. She had created a world of opulence and comfort he felt proud to come home to. Why did it suddenly feel so empty?

"Constance?"

"Yes?" She looked slightly annoyed, and he realized he'd interrupted her in the middle of a story.

"I'm going to check on Muffy."

"I'm sure she's all right, dear. She's probably sleeping."

He felt a flash of rage, a long-buried emotion, and it surprised him.

"I'll go up just the same."

He ignored the puzzled look on her face and pushed his chair away from the table. For some reason he couldn't quite define, he didn't want to be around Constance's friends tonight, with their gossip and chattering. Their endless little social games.

Solitude would have been preferable. But more than anything, he hoped his daughter would be awake and might want to talk to him.

John walked slowly up the huge staircase, then down the long hall, flanked with the delicate antique tables and huge vases Constance adored, until he reached his daughter's bedroom door.

As he was just about to knock, he heard the first sob. It was a small, stifled sound, and it tore at his heart.

He stood in the hallway, his hand upraised, then slowly lowered his arm and stared at the door.

Muffy had been an extremely private child, and she hadn't changed as she had grown up. If he walked in on her now, it would be excruciatingly embarrassing for her. Almost painful.

Confused, he stepped silently away from the door and began to walk toward his own bedroom. Funny how he'd never questioned Constance when she had insisted she needed a bedroom of her own. She had decorated his exquisitely. It was a soothing room. But tonight it would offer him no comfort.

MUFFY TRIED TO STOP the next sob by holding her hand tightly over her mouth, but it exploded out of her. She turned her head into the down pillow and began to cry.

Where was Phillip when she needed him? She couldn't wait until three days before the wedding. She had to talk to him now.

Her hand strayed downward, until it rested protectively over her stomach. She'd first suspected when she'd been so tired in the mornings. Then the nausea. Thank God her mother rarely came into her room and usually saw her for the first time at the breakfast table.

There was no possible way of explaining this to her mother without Constance becoming absolutely enraged. All of her plans would be spoiled, all her desires thwarted, if she knew her perfect daughter was already almost three months pregnant with Phillip's baby.

Muffy's eyes filled with tears again. So frightened, so terribly scared, and there was absolutely no one she could confide in. No one she wanted to tell.

Except Phillip.

Closing her eyes as two more tears slid down the sides of her face and into her ears, Elizabeth Ann "Muffy" Bradford wondered exactly how she was going to make it through the next few weeks.

Chapter Ten

"You seem a little nervous today, Alex. Is it something I've done?"

Sean had been carefully keeping track of Alex's emotional state since his talk with Charlie over Thanksgiving. Much of what he'd revealed made the things Alex did or said so much more comprehensible. Sean ached at the thought that she had ever considered herself not quite good enough, that she'd ever thought there was something wrong with her.

But now, with Phillip coming home within the week, he'd be able to tell her the entire truth before the wedding. Once he had Phillip's permission to let Alex in on the secret, he would tell her.

"No. I'm having dinner with my mother, and I'm just a little tired, that's all."

He knew it was so much more, but he refrained from saying anything. Some things had to be earned, and he hadn't earned that right from Alex yet. But once the wedding was over and Phillip had been revealed as the true groom... Then Sean planned on asking Alex to spend the rest of her life with him. He was going to go all the way, with a ring, a bottle of champagne, down on bended knee, whatever it took to win her heart.

In a way, though, their relationship had had such severe constraints placed upon it, and both of them had stood a rather peculiar test of time. They'd had a few quiet dinners together, talked about what mattered to both of them, told each other what they wanted out of life.

He'd found out that Alex wasn't a burned-out career woman, that her feelings ran quite contrary to the stereotype. She loved her job and loved the Biltmore. For the Biltmore Hotel was not a hotel in the accepted sense of the word. It was a place that was totally unique. Alex didn't do simple conventions for tractor salesmen or the Elks Club.

One night she might be orchestrating a reception for the People's Republic of China in honor of the opening of their new consulate office in Los Angeles. Another evening, she might be in charge of a concert fund-raiser for the Music Center Opera starring various musical celebrities, and setting up a dessert buffet—a Viennese table loaded down with delectables, including a completely edible chocolate cart cascading with dipped strawberries. On still another night the former prime minster of Japan and two hundred and eighty guests might arrive for dinner.

It wasn't an ordinary job, and she was certainly not an ordinary woman. She didn't dislike her job, she'd simply thought there were parts of her life that weren't in balance, and one of those parts had been having someone to love.

She was just as much in love with her chosen profession as he was. In that way, they certainly complemented each other. He found almost nothing more exciting than making the deal, taking a building and making it over, watching a piece of architecture reach its full potential.

He'd spent an entire evening telling her all about his life after his father had died and left the family business in his children's hands. Sean was the oldest, with a younger sister named Jessica and a younger brother, Brian. Sean had refused to admit defeat in those early years and had driven himself relentlessly in his desire to keep the construction business in the family and learn as much as he possibly could.

He'd been impressed by Alex's education. Swiss boarding schools and universities in both London and Paris. She'd been touched by his longing to finish his formal education. He'd had to drop out of school when his father died, but he had always wanted to go back and finish. There had never been time.

What came easiest to him was being dynamic and making the deal. Patience was in short supply. This time he'd spent with Alex had certainly taught him the value of waiting patiently for what one truly wanted.

She had been an expert in learning the rules and acting carefully, cautiously, accordingly. But she'd always wanted to be more instinctual, to throw away the rule book and follow her feelings. Once she had fallen in love with Sean, she'd had no choice.

But perhaps the real miracle was that a terribly romantic man who had become a total cynic concerning the opposite sex and a woman who had felt that she was destined to spend her life alone with no passionate feeling for a man had somehow found each other and, in learning how to love each other, brought out the best each had to give.

"Where are you and your mother going out to dinner?"

"Morton's."

There was still a touch of wariness in her eyes, as if she believed their relationship was all going to be taken away from her at the stroke of midnight. And each time he might have become impatient with her, Sean remembered she was risking far more than he was. After all, he already knew exactly what the Bradford wedding was all about.

All he had to do was think of her as a small child, being bundled from house to house, and his heart went out to her. He had made a silent vow, after the talk with Charlie, to do everything in his power to see that the world didn't hurt Alex once they were together.

He lay awake at nights, hoping he hadn't put her through too much pain. Hoping that she would understand he had made a promise to a friend and had had to see it out to the end.

As for the wedding ... Muffy looked like a total wreck, Constance was beginning to get shrewish and snap just the tiniest bit, John Bradford seemed to know that something wasn't quite right, and Phillip ...

Sean smiled as he left Alex's office, his hands in his pockets and a certain jauntiness to his walk. Phillip would be here Wednesday night. According to their plan, he would head straight for Sean's house, and when he did, Sean was going to get his friend to grant him permission to confide in Alex. Then, however late the hour, he was going to take her out for a very special dinner.

Life was looking very good, indeed.

MORTON'S WAS very much like the Meredith Michaels Alex had slowly come to know. Though there was an ever-present lineup of Mercedeses and Rolls-Royces outside, inside the restaurant was as casual as it was elegant. The staff was friendly, the decor comfortable, and the atmosphere was decidedly unstuffy.

Alex enjoyed the tropical feel of the restaurant, enhanced by the warm pink walls and palm trees. She also thought the restaurant's hot-fudge sundaes were the best in the city.

Once they had ordered—Alex, the marinated grilled lamb, her mother, the grilled chicken breast with black bean puree and tomatillo-and-avocado salsa—both women leaned back in their chairs and sipped their wine.

The truth was, both were afraid to make the first move.

Meredith had never forgiven herself for relinquishing her baby daughter at the age of six weeks, and Alex had never wanted to pry into her mother's reasoning, as she was deathly afraid something had been wrong with her. Meredith was just as afraid that her daughter would never forgive her.

Thus, Alex had learned, over the years, to treat her
mother in a manner very similar to that in which she treated
her clients. And Meredith didn't have the faintest idea what
to do with her daughter.

The only time a real mother-daughter exchange occurred
was when Meredith asked her daughter about her love life.

And tonight was no exception.

They chatted about inconsequential things through most
of the dinner.

"Your father's putting on weight. I'm worried about
him."

"Have you seen that new book out on cholesterol,
Mother? Maybe you could give it to your cook, and she
could sneak in a few recipes."

"Your hair looks very pretty tonight, Alexandra. I like it
pulled back in a braid. You have such a beautiful face."

"Marcy did it for me. Do you like the bow?"

"It's charming."

Love me.

Forgive me.

"Your father and I gave a dinner party the other night,
and one of the women expressed an interest in Karin's
painting. Is she going to have another showing soon?"

"The end of February. I'll keep you posted."

"This salsa is delicious. Would you like to try some?"

"Sure. Pierre will want a whole breakdown of this dinner tomorrow, what was served with what. He gets such
great ideas when we talk about food."

After dinner and over coffee, Meredith asked the inevi-
table question.

"Have you been seeing anyone special?"

Taking a deep breath, Alex nodded her head.

Meredith's coffee cup stopped midway to her lips. She
attempted a smile then, and her mouth quivered. And as
Alex looked at her mother, she knew she would remember

the way her mother looked, at that exact moment, the rest of her life.

There was something between them, after all.

"Oh, Alex. Do you think—"

"I don't know." And Alex, always emotionally overloaded when she visited with her mother, felt her eyes begin to fill.

Meredith set down her coffee then, and leaned toward her daughter. "Are you unsure about him?"

"Not at all."

"Is there . . . is there another . . ."

"Yes."

"Oh." Meredith glanced back down at her coffee cup, then picked it up and took another sip.

And Alex noticed her mother's hands. Meredith took great pride in her personal appearance in the way that wealthy women do when it's all they have left. Now, for the first time, Alex saw the tiny age spots, the slightly wrinkled skin. For some reason it made her think of her mother as incredibly vulnerable.

"I don't know how things are going to work out and—I hate not knowing."

"I remember that rule book. You had to have it." A genuine smile curved her mother's perfectly-glossed lips. "It's too bad that there aren't any rules when it comes to love."

"I don't know." Alex watched as their waiter poured them each another cup of coffee, then she leaned forward again, reaching for the cream. "There's not much to say. Where did you get that bracelet? I really like it."

"Alex."

"It goes so well with your earrings."

"Alex, just let me say something. Please."

Alex looked down at her coffee, concentrating on stirring in just the right amount of sugar.

"I haven't been much of a mother to you, I know. There's no possible excuse for what I did. But I've been doing a lot of thinking. You remember Betsy Taylor?"

Betsy Taylor. Her mother's best friend. Shopping companion and confidante. Married to another wealthy man many years her senior, Betsy was probably the closest thing to family Meredith had ever had.

"I remember Betsy."

"She died last month."

"You never told me."

"I couldn't. It took me long enough to accept the fact that she was gone. But I've been thinking a lot, Alex, and if there's one thing I could do over with my life, it would be take more chances. All of my life I've been so afraid. Of your father. Of you—"

"Me!"

"I was scared when I brought you home. The way all new mothers are. I didn't know what to do. And James—when he didn't have things the way he wanted them, he could be very cold."

This was emotionally loaded ground, and Alex could feel her legs starting to shake, her throat closing up.

"Why did you do it?"

Meredith looked away.

"No." Alex took her hand. "Look at me. Why did you do it?"

Meredith suddenly seemed very, very old and tired. "When you were born and I brought you home— Alex, I was also overjoyed. I thought my life was complete. You were a beautiful child, so warm, so loving. But James hated the intrusion. He was jealous of you, jealous of the time I spent with you, even jealous when I breast-fed you.

"The trip to London was an ultimatum. He wanted me with him, or... that was it. Colleen knew your father well. She'd heard all about him from Charlie. She suggested that

I leave you with her. She'd had two miscarriages and a still-birth and wanted a baby to hold so badly.''

"I didn't know that.''

"She never talks about it. I was at the hospital after the stillbirth, and believe me, Charlie was completely out of his head. He thought he was losing her, right in front of his eyes.''

Alex let go of her mother's hand, sensing the story was well under way and knowing she was going to hear the truth.

"When we came back from London, I brought you home. James wasn't pleased. Babies were such an inconvenience to him. I didn't realize, before we were married, that he would be the only child in our marriage. Five days later he told me we were going to New York. He told me to pack my bags and make arrangements for you. I took you to Colleen again.

"This went on for almost six months. When I came back from that last business trip, Charlie let me into the house. I walked into the den, and you were sitting in your aunt's lap next to the fire. She didn't see me, but I will never forget the look on your face. You were smiling up at Colleen with every bit of happiness in your tiny body, and I knew then that I had lost you.''

Alex sat perfectly still, knowing that if she moved she would burst into tears.

"Charlie caught up with me on the way to the car, and we had a long talk. I had made them your godparents when you were baptized because they had been so kind to me when I married your father. I was at my wit's end trying to save my marriage . . .''

Her voice trailed off, and she was silent for a moment, then said quietly, "And the irony of it all was, I wasn't able to save it. Don't look so shocked, Alex. I'd have to be blind not to know he has other women. I was a fool to believe I couldn't have worked out something on my own. Charlie and Colleen would have helped me. But James was everything to me, then.''

Alex dug her fingernails into her palms and willed her heart to stop racing. Then slowly, ever so slowly, she asked the question she had to have an answer to.

''Was there anything . . . *wrong* with me?''

''Darling, no! I was simply an immature nineteen-year-old who was desperately in love with an older man and foolish enough to think I could change him. But when I saw you smiling at Colleen . . . I knew it was unfair to keep moving you from home to home. I think I also knew James would never change. I made the decision I made . . . selfishly, because I wanted to keep my husband. But I also wanted what was best for you, and you couldn't have had a better substitute mother than Colleen. She *is* your mother, Alex.''

Meredith looked away then, her eyes brimming, her hands clasped tightly together. Alex could see she was visibly struggling to regain control of her emotions.

When Meredith finally continued, her voice was low. ''I lost you, and I lost him. And I regret both the losses and know exactly what kind of fool I was. Right before Betsy died . . . we talked, Alex, like we had never talked before. I made up my mind over the last few weeks. I didn't want to wait until one of us was dying to talk about it. I didn't want to die and leave you wondering what had happened. I couldn't have faced death knowing we'd never talked about what had happened.''

''Nineteen,'' Alex said softly. A lifetime ago. She'd been in Paris, thinking she was so sophisticated, yet knowing nothing of the world. *Would I have done that much better? Could I have stood up to James at that age?*

Never.

''I don't expect forgiveness from you, Alex. Not when I can't forgive myself. But I just want to say don't do what I did. I lost a child and a husband simply because I was too scared to do what I knew was right for me. Not morally right, but *right*. Do you understand what it is I'm trying to say?"

"I think so."

"If this man is right for you, be brave and make him yours. Whatever you want in the world, Alex, have the courage to go after it. I've always been so proud of the way you made a life for yourself out from underneath your father. You did what I couldn't."

Alex was silent, taking this all in. She had to admire her mother's courage. She had always wanted to have a talk like this with Meredith, and though it had been one of the most painful and grueling experiences she'd ever had, she was glad it was finally out in the open.

But she didn't know if she could take much more.

Apparently, neither did Meredith.

"I've paid the check already, Alex. I'm going to go now, and...thank you for listening to me. I hope things work out with this man of yours." She was talking rapidly, and was almost starting to rise out of her chair when Alex put her hand over her mother's.

"Thank you. Thank you."

"I've never said it," Meredith whispered as she got to her feet, "but you were a joy to watch growing up. I'm so proud of you, Alex. You must know that."

After her mother had gone, Alex signaled the waiter for another cup of coffee, then drank it slowly, staring blindly ahead.

In all of her wildest fantasies, she'd never thought she and her mother would discuss life, death and their relationship over dinner at Morton's.

Life was truly amazing.

SEAN PICKED UP on the second ring.

"Alex?" he said softly. There were two lines in the penthouse, and she was the only one who knew the number of the one that had rung.

"Hi. I . . . just wanted to talk with you for a little bit."

"You never have to give me an excuse to call. I love talking with you."

There was a short pause, then he said, "How did your dinner go?"

"All right."

He sensed so much more, but wasn't about to pry.

There was another short silence, then Sean decided to ask her directly. "Alex, have you ever felt that I thought you weren't good enough for me?"

"Sometimes."

"I want you to know that you're wrong."

"I hope so."

She's not feeling well.

"Are you free the evening of the seventeenth?"

"I will be around ten."

"Can I take you out to dinner?"

"I don't think so. What if someone saw us, right before the wedding?"

"Would you come to dinner here, then?"

"All right."

It was all he could offer her for now, and he chafed at the restrictions in his life.

"It's going to be all right, Alex. I wish things had been different up to now, but it's going to turn out just fine."

"I guess I just needed to hear you say it."

Her voice was tight, the sound painful to his ears.

"It will be, darling. It will be."

"WHAT DO YOU MEAN I can't leave tomorrow! I have to be in Los Angeles the evening of the seventeenth!" Phillip faced three of the security guards in their gray suit pants, white shirts and navy blazers.

"It's orders. Colonel Brimley has to open the bidding, and he's snowed in up at his vacation house in New Hampshire."

"Look," Phillip said quietly, hearing and hating the note of quiet desperation in his voice. "You cannot keep me here against my will. I'm leaving, and none of you can stop me."

"Phil, be reasonable. We're miles from the nearest pay phone. This location was chosen specifically because of its isolation. You couldn't make it to the airport in time if you started walking right now."

"All right. All right." All he could think about was Muffy and what she would go through if he didn't show up on time and as planned. "There has to be a suitable compromise."

"There isn't one. There's only this. You can't leave this farmhouse until the bidding commences, and it isn't going to start unless Brimley gets to Washington."

Phillip could feel Rachel's sympathetic gaze, and it was more than he could bear. There was no way out. The sky had been slate gray and ominous earlier this evening, and now a heavy rain was falling. You could barely see outside the windows. The news had predicted sleet later on, and possibly snow. The farmhouse was surrounded by thick woods, and even if he made it to a main road, they were a couple of hours from the nearest airport.

He was trapped.

"When do they think Brimley will make it down?" he asked, fighting the feelings of panic. *If Muffy cracks, if Constance finds out...*

"Things are looking good for the next day or so. You won't be that late."

He turned to Rachel. Rachel, of the calm mind and rational outlook. Rachel might have something useful to add to this nightmarish conversation.

"Let's take a look at the news, Phil. And hope that the weather doesn't get any worse."

Chapter Eleven

Alex knew, the minute she saw Sean's face on the evening of the seventeenth, that something was very wrong.

He led her into the suite and shut the door behind her.

"Alex, this is going to be very hard to explain."

She felt her hands start to turn to ice, her throat start to close. Her worst fears were becoming reality. In a minute her eyes would be stinging and she'd be ready to burst into tears.

She'd heard this particular speech before. She'd just never expected to hear it from Sean.

Constance Bulldozer Bradford had put Alex through the wringer today, and she had looked forward to a nice, quiet dinner with Sean. She had been on an emotional high all day, because from everything her instincts were telling her, this dinner was going to be different.

Well, it's different, all right. To hell with instincts. Just let me get out of here before I try to murder this man.

"What's going to be hard to explain?"

"Well, the hardest part is that I can't explain it to you just now."

"I don't understand," she said quietly, her hands crossed in front of her chest as if they could hold in all the pain in the world. "All this week, you've been acting as if tonight was going to be something very special, and now you can't explain anything to me?"

She took a deep breath. *Be brave. Fight for what you want.* "Sean, I can't keep being in the dark about what we have, hoping for something that might happen. I want to know if there's anything for us in the future. I want that, but I'm not sure if you do."

"I do!"

"Then trust me. *Tell me what's going on.*"

He looked at her for a long moment, then slowly let out his breath. "I can't. I'm sorry, Alex, but I just can't."

"You ask me to trust you, but you can't trust me."

"There are other people involved. I made a promise."

After all they'd had, the words she used to end it were so inconsequential.

"I'm tired, Sean. I think I'm going home."

She was so tired that she walked in the wrong direction, directly into the dining alcove. And what she saw made her want to weep.

The small table was set with some of the Biltmore's prettiest china. Candles glowed, crystal sparkled. The meal hadn't arrived yet, but it was obvious Sean had gone to a lot of trouble to prepare a special evening for the two of them.

A special evening she didn't want to share with him. It was all too much. The dinner with her mother earlier in the week. The months of pressure leading up to this wedding. The last-minute preparations. Meeting Sean, the intense attraction between them and finding out he was everything she'd ever wanted in a man.

And couldn't have.

She turned to face him. He'd been behind her, watching her from the doorway into the dining alcove.

"I can't," she said, her voice choked with tears.

"I know," he said softly, and it was worse than if he'd yelled at her or tried to make excuses or begged her to reconsider.

"I'm just so tired, Sean."

"It's all right, Alex."

"I can't do this anymore." Her voice broke, and she started to cry. "I don't want you to be with anyone else. I want you to be with me, and you can't be with me, can you?"

"Not yet." His voice sounded so infinitely sad.

"I'm going home," she said softly.

"I'll drive you."

"No."

"Yes. You're in no shape to drive."

Room service chose just that moment to arrive, and while Alex washed her face and pulled herself together in the bathroom, Sean instructed the waiter to leave the trolley by the small table.

When she came out, he'd opened one of the trays and had put it on the floor for Roscoe. It looked like salmon.

"Ready to go?"

She nodded.

He held her hand all the way home. Somehow that made things all the more sad. Sean saw her to her door, and as Alex heard the car drive off down the street, she woodenly climbed the stairs to her bedroom. Not even bothering to take off her clothes, she kicked off her heels and crawled into bed.

PHILLIP, WHERE THE HELL are you?

Sean drove swiftly back to the Biltmore, then checked the answering machine in his house in Malibu.

Nothing.

He'd been checking since six this evening, when he'd driven to LAX to pick up his friend and he hadn't been on the flight they had agreed on.

Less than seventy-two hours until the wedding, and the real groom was nowhere to be found.

Sean kept a tight control over his emotions. All his energy was focused on how he was going to solve this mess and make sure things were all right between him and Alex.

Lying in bed that night, emotionally exhausted, Sean sat up slowly and rubbed his open palm over his face.

Muffy. She'll have to be told. He thought of stalling her, pretending Phillip had arrived. Muffy wouldn't believe him. She'd been acting kind of strange lately, and Sean had a sudden vision of her simply collapsing and telling her mother everything.

And it would be all over. Constance had dominated the girl from the day she was born and would have no trouble shipping her off somewhere.

One thing he was absolutely sure of. Phillip would have to have one hell of an excuse.

"YOU'VE GOT TO let me go. My friend has money, lots of it. How much do you want for a set of car keys?" Phillip knew he was close to groveling, but he couldn't help himself.

The guard shook his head slowly, still chewing on a grilled cheese sandwich that Rachel had made him.

"For God's sake, it's not just me I'm thinking about. There are other people involved."

"Can't. Orders are orders."

It was hopeless. The rain had turned first to sleet and now to snow. All Phillip could see out any of the farmhouse windows was an endless vista of white. He wandered into the living room, just in time to hear the weather report.

"Heavy snows predicted in the northeast and mid-Atlantic states for tonight, and more tomorrow." The blonde in a royal-blue tailored blouse looked as perky and cheerful as a cheerleader.

He finally understood why Elvis had made a hobby out of shooting television screens.

"Phil."

It was Rachel, coming down the stairs.

"I talked one of the guys into calling the national weather report hotline, and he said the man in charge believes the snow is going to let up by the twentieth."

"That's cutting it awfully close."

"I'm afraid close is all you've got right now."

"ALEX, THAT'S ONE sharp dress."

"Thanks, Marcy."

It was a classic dress that she used a lot, and it never failed to receive compliments. A black chemise style, it had a low-cut back filled in with sheer black lace. The skirt came right to the middle of her knees. With sheer black hose and black heels, it was an extremely elegant look.

Perfect for the director of catering. Perfect for the last of the Bradford parties, on the eve of Sean's wedding to Muffy.

She'd thought about coming down with some exotic disease. She'd thought about asking Marcy to go in her place. But as the person who had coordinated everything and, in the end, had to pull this entire thing off, Alex couldn't do it.

There was such a thing as professional pride.

And there was such a thing as no pride at all. She desperately wanted to see Sean one more time before he became Muffy's husband.

Marcy eyed her critically. "Darker lipstick."

"You think so?"

She nodded. "Black is terrific on you, but if you don't go darker on your mouth, you're going to look washed out."

If there was one bright spot among this entire mess, it was seeing Marcy develop professionally. Her outfits had become only slightly less outrageous since the day she took over Louise's job, and Alex had been getting nothing but positive feedback from her clients.

These days Marcy looked more like a businesswoman, a classicist and a debutante than a catwoman, gypsy or movie star. Alex was sure she still saved her more flamboyant looks for evening, but during the day Marcy looked every inch the professional.

Alex had stopped outside her office one day and observed Marcy through the large plate-glass window. She had been looking around her small office space as if it were the Taj Mahal.

Those were the days. The way Alex felt right now, she could be given the ownership of the entire hotel and it wouldn't mean a thing.

"Are you okay?"

Marcy's question brought Alex back to the present moment with a start. Her new assistant caterer had a sharp eye, but Alex had kept the news of her break with Sean totally private. It was still too new, too raw.

"Just tired. I'll be glad to get Mrs. Bradford off my back."

"I'm going to be working in the office this Saturday, catching up on some work. Buzz me if you need anything, all right?"

"I promise."

Once Marcy had left, Alex took a good look at herself in the mirror.

You do look too pale. She put on a darker lipstick, then stepped back a little to see the entire effect.

She looked wonderful.

She felt miserable.

She tried a smile in the mirror, and her lips quivered.

Come on.

The next smile wasn't as pathetic.

It's show time.

MUFFY'S HANDS were like ice.

"Where is he?" she whispered as Sean led her to a corner of the spacious Gold Room.

"I don't know. Something must have come up at Stealthco. But I'm sure he'll be here in time for the wedding."

"Sean, what do we do if he's not here? What can we say?"

She was looking at him as if he had the answers to the world's problems tattooed on his forehead. He loved Phillip like a brother, but Sean couldn't help contrasting Muffy with Alex. Muffy was a woman a man would have to protect and care for for the rest of his life. Alex was a fighter. She would stand next to the man she loved and help him face anything life flung their way.

With the exception of his marrying another woman.

He could understand that. She'd been remarkably understanding. Wonderful. He couldn't blame her for being angry at the thought of him marrying another woman.

He saw her the moment she walked into the ballroom.

Just like that first night in her office, she completely took his breath away.

The black dress was fitted, skimming her curves. He liked the style. A woman had to be truly striking to wear a dress like that to its best advantage. She'd coiled her hair on top of her head. It was a striking foil to her bone structure, the high cheekbones and square, strong jaw.

But her mouth... It had intrigued him from the first. Tonight it was boldly colored, sharply defined against her understated makeup.

He looked to his heart's content. But when she glanced his way, he couldn't bring himself to meet her gaze. *She trusted you. And you betrayed that trust.*

"Sean. Sean!" The whisper had a tinge of desperation. "My mother's coming this way!"

As much as he longed to go to Alex and tell her the truth, he couldn't. Not until Phillip arrived. If he was totally honest with himself, he'd admit he was just as nervous as Muffy was. The wedding was tomorrow at three in the afternoon. There were eight hundred people invited, the cream of both New York and Los Angeles society. The rich and famous and powerful.

Over fifty people were going to be dressed in Renaissance costumes. There was a table that ran the length of the

Crystal Ballroom that would be groaning beneath the weight of all the sumptuous dishes piled high on it. Of course, the Bradfords' minister was overseeing the ceremony. There was a small string quartet complete with a harpist. And his brother Brian was filling in as best man—though Brian knew nothing about the deception involved, but after this was all over he would surely understand.

Almost every woman Sean had ever been involved with would be attending this wedding. Most wouldn't have missed it, curious to see him finally get caught, as they so graphically put it. Many of his father's friends were on the guest list. He'd probably easily know over half the guests.

Hell, he'd even invited some of them to make this whole thing seem real enough to Constance. Phil had given him a list of people he wanted attending this wedding. They had numerous friends in common, so it hadn't been hard for their lists to overlap. Sean had simply asked his secretary to type up his guest list and he'd given it to Constance.

But just what was he going to do, if Phillip didn't show up before the minister asked him if he was going to have and to hold, love and cherish, till death do us part?

Nothing like making a total ass out of yourself in front of a cast of thousands.

The strangest thing was, there was only one woman's opinion that counted. And at this moment she thought he was lower than a snake's belly.

He loved her. Alexandra Michaels had given him so much. Most important, she'd given him back the ability to feel deeply and to believe that a woman could love a man for what he was as opposed to what he had in a Swiss bank.

He'd known the moment he'd started talking to her that it was over. Temporarily. The fact that she had told him the truth instead of screaming, raving and ranting had endeared her to him even more. She had simply let him know she couldn't take any more of not knowing. He had understood, wondering all the while if he would have been as understanding as she'd been if their roles had been reversed.

He didn't think so.

"Hello, Sean."

Constance. Muffy was clinging to his arm as if it were a lifeline.

"Hello, Constance."

"Ready for tomorrow?"

She looked so pleased with herself. He wanted to throttle her. But, suppressing his baser instincts, he smiled down at her.

"As ready as I'll ever be."

"You won't change your mind about the morning suit?" Typical Constance, always trying to get her way, even at the end.

"No." Even if he felt like a clown, at least he didn't have to look like one.

As he watched the way her blue eyes narrowed, he thought what a pity it was that they weren't in Switzerland on a ski trip and this woman wasn't directly in the path of an avalanche.

"Well, I'll leave the two of you to mingle, and I'll see you tomorrow, Sean."

Yes, indeedy.

He glanced up right at that moment and caught Alex looking at him. Their eyes locked and held until a blush rose in her face and she looked away, her eyes dark and glistening.

And Sean wondered, for the first time in his life, if he'd found the deal he just couldn't make.

ALEX GLANCED AWAY, furious with herself that he'd caught her looking at him.

And, ignoring all protocol, when it came to overseeing a party of this importance, she walked over to the bar where

Tony was mixing drinks and working his own special blend of magic.

"Perrier with a twist, Alex?"

"Something stronger."

One thing she loved about Tony was that he was just about as unjudgmental as a bartender could be, and that was definitely pretty unjudgmental. He was a sharp dresser, and she employed him for her most important parties time and time again because he was handsome, talented, knew how to talk to people and could mix a drink faster than anyone she knew.

"Any preferences?"

"Surprise me."

The drink he handed her was long, cool and tropical—with a lethal kick to it and a tiny paper umbrella. Trust Tony to have a sense of humor.

"This'll do it." She took a long swig out of the tall, frosted glass as she started across the room. Her father, James, was a four-vodka-martini-per-business-lunch man, and Alex had inherited his tolerance for liquor. She didn't drink a lot, mostly socially, but this was an occasion that merited getting soused.

What a world.

Now, in one of those romance novels in which this would have been a marriage of convenience, she would know exactly what to do. Cool and regal, lightning-fast with the witty comeback, she would be thrusting and parrying conversational sparklers with her hero, making him realize there was only one woman in the world he could ever love.

But the way these things really happened was the way they were happening now. Sean and Muffy were in the center of the room, surrounded by throngs of well-wishers, and she was on the sidelines, drinking a tropical bomb.

That about sums things up.

She glanced at her watch. Only an hour to go, and then she could legitimately leave. And leave she would. She was spending the night in her room at the hotel. The suit she was wearing to the wedding was already hanging in the closet. She'd order up a dinner, leave it untouched, turn on the television and hope there was a nice, comforting sitcom on the nostalgia channel like *Mr. Ed* or the *Donna Reed Show.* Maybe even *Gilligan's Island.* She'd stare at the screen, not sleep a wink and come downstairs to the Crystal Ballroom tomorrow looking like hell and feeling worse.

Good game plan. I approve.

But for now, she had—Alex glanced at her watch again— fifty-eight more minutes of this to get through.

TO HELL WITH IT. Tell her the truth. How angry can Phillip get? She won't tell anyone—

"Sean?" The voice was so very soft, almost a whisper.

"What is it, Muffy?"

"I don't feel so good. I think I need some air."

And with that, she fainted.

ALEX ALMOST CHOKED on her paper umbrella when she heard the murmur of the crowd and saw Sean sweep Muffy up into his arms. The girl's head was hanging limply, her color was bad, and her mother was furious.

And Sean cut a wide swathe through the crowd, straight toward her.

Well, isn't that why you're here? To make sure everything goes smoothly?

"Where can she lie down?"

"Take her to my room."

And with Constance following them like a shark who smelled blood, Alex led the way to the elevator and up to her room.

Once Muffy was on Alex's bed, Sean sitting beside her and stroking the fine blond hair off her forehead, Constance exploded.

"Look what she's doing to me! What is *wrong* with her. This is the wedding every girl dreams of having, and she faints at her own party! She's the most ungrateful—"

Alex watched the woman spew her venom and realized if Constance Bradford's facade was starting to crumble, they were all in big trouble.

"Mrs. Bradford, why don't you go downstairs and see to your guests? Sean, why don't you go with her?"

As she turned toward Sean, she murmured, "Get her out of here."

Sean looked worried. "One of the guests is a doctor. I'll send him up."

Alex simply nodded, her eyes on Muffy.

In record time, Sean and Constance were out of the room.

Alex called room service and ordered up some hot tea, a 7-Up and some orange juice. Muffy could have a choice when she came to.

The girl was sitting up in bed and sipping the 7-Up when the doctor arrived.

Alex moved away from the bed to give them privacy. She could still hear bits and pieces of the conversation.

"Anything you could have been allergic to?"

"No."

"Have you fainted before?"

"No."

Muffy looked so pathetic in her crumpled pink party dress, her thin blond hair straggling around her neck. She'd been wearing her hair up, Alex suspected, in a pitiful attempt to seem older. Now, as it fell around her face, she looked about twelve years old instead of twenty-one.

Alex's heart went out to her.

She wasn't even given the satisfaction of hating the other woman. This was no hussy dressed in scarlet with a cigarette dangling from her brightly painted lips. This was a pathetic little girl, with a monster of a mother, marrying a man who didn't even love her.

And then, the million dollar question.

"Could you be pregnant?" The doctor's voice was gentle.

Muffy paused just that one second too long, then covered her face and whispered, "Please don't tell my mother."

And Alex felt the blood leave her face in a rush as it began to roar in her ears. She grasped the edge of the table, steadying herself as she lowered her shaking body into a chair.

Pregnant?

"How far along are you?"

"Almost four months."

Three months. You met Sean three months ago. They must have announced their engagement the second she missed her period.

"Have you been eating well, getting enough rest?"

Muffy started to cry. "I'm just so scared." The words were choked out of her.

"And the father? Is he—" And here the doctor hesitated, choosing his words carefully as he comforted the crying girl. "Is he the sort of man who's going to be there for you?"

"Oh, yes." Muffy hiccupped. "He's so wonderful, so loyal, it's just that—" And she dissolved into another bout of sobbing.

Alex felt her eyes filling. She remembered Sean's words. *And if I told you it had everything to do with loyalty and nothing to do with love—*

If this had been one of those romance novels, *she* would have been the one in bed confessing to a pregnancy, and the hero would have been by her side, a thunderstruck expression on his face.

Well, at least now you know Sean's secret. He's nothing if not loyal. Loyalty's a good thing in a man. Okay, so she's pregnant. Oh, what the hell. The rich and famous are different. I mean, look at my own mother, who gave me over

*to Colleen and made her my mother. Maybe Muffy can
mother his child and I can be his wife. Maybe we could all
live together in that big house out in Malibu, and maybe I'm
just quietly losing my mind....*

"Can you stay with her?"

Alex blinked and realized the doctor was speaking to her.

"Of course." She made up her mind, in that instant, that
no matter what she was feeling, she could not possibly take
it out on Muffy.

"I want her to rest until the wedding." He lowered his
voice so that Muffy couldn't hear. "She's a high-strung little thing, and there's a very real possibility she could lose the
baby. Am I making myself perfectly clear?"

Alex nodded.

"Here's my number. I'm going downstairs to tell Constance her daughter is all right."

"Don't bother."

His dark eyes were shrewd, and Alex saw understanding
in them. So he knew Constance for what she really was as
well as she did.

"I'll be at the wedding tomorrow. Don't hesitate to call
me if you need help. I don't care what time it is."

"Thank you."

He left, then Alex went and sat in the overstuffed chair
next to the bed and watched Muffy sleep. She was so thin,
so pale, it seemed impossible she could be carrying a child.

*Now, this is more like one of those novels. Jilted heroine
with the other woman who's pregnant and could lose the
baby if she doesn't stay quiet. If I was a heroine worth my
salt, she'd be up doing the mambo—*

But she couldn't. Even the joke fell flat in her mind.

Muffy was just too helpless.

*But there's another person involved in this, two to tango
and all that. He's not helpless. Far from it.*

She was determined that before the night was over, she

was going to pay Sean Lawton a little visit.

And tell him exactly what she thought of him.

"SEAN? ALEX. Could I come up and see you for just a second?"

"Of course."

Muffy slept for almost an hour. When she woke, she swore Alex to secrecy. And Alex had promised she wouldn't tell a soul, but she had to tell Sean what she thought of him. That wasn't really telling because he already knew.

She could forgive him for getting Muffy pregnant before he knew her. She even thought it was kind of admirable of him to go through with the wedding in the first place, to give his child a name. A lot of today's new males wouldn't have bothered.

But what she would never forgive him for was letting her believe they had a future together. Even with the peculiar sense of morality known only to the very rich, what Sean had obviously had in mind was totally untenable to her.

With Marcy watching Muffy, Alex took the elevator up to the Presidential Suite.

SEAN WAS waiting for her.

She walked all the way into the large bedroom, then turned and stared at him.

So much for instincts. Maybe the library will let me have my books back.

"How's Muffy?"

At least he was concerned about her.

"Fine. I just—" She took a deep breath. She'd wanted to tell him off all evening, so why did she feel so awful? "I just want you to know that she told me everything. I know what's going on now."

"You do?" He seemed incredulous.

"Yes. Loyalty and all that. Why you're going ahead with this wedding. All the pieces fell into place, Sean. You're nothing if not loyal."

"Alex." His eyes darkened, then before she knew what was happening, he'd crossed the room and pulled her into his arms.

"I thought I'd lost you. I couldn't tell you what was going on. You understand that now, don't you? But now we can be together. I don't ever want us to be apart again."

Her brain was shutting down, but she had just enough sanity left to dig the stiletto heel of her black pump into his foot.

"Ahhh!"

That got his attention.

He released her, then grabbed his foot and began hopping around the room, his face a grimace of pain.

"Pig with a capital P!" she shouted. Then, because this man had succeeded in driving her completely out of her mind, lowering all her defenses and breaking down every bit of her normal, rational sense of control, she pushed him over onto the big bed, watching him land in the middle of the mattress with a resounding thwack.

"Just what in God's name did you *think* I was going to do when I found out?"

"Alex, I realize it was a bit of deception, but none of it was meant maliciously—"

"Oh, no, just schmooze me along, Alex the idiot. You let me think we had some kind of future together, when all the time you *knew*—"

"Of course I knew. I wouldn't have done it if I hadn't known—"

"Answer me this, then, smart guy. Where are we all going to live? In your house in Malibu? And what's the next step in your illustrious career, running for political office? You should, you know, if you fooled me you could fool the entire country, and we could have a *pig* in the White House!''

"Alex, what are you—''

"I may be naive, but I'm *not* stupid! I will *not* play your rich little games or move people around like pawns on a chessboard. What were you doing, lining me up for the last few months so you could be assured of having a continual good time in bed? Just what did you think you could do, buy me off with a blank check like the rest of the bimbos you've obviously been with?''

"Alex, you don't understand—''

"No, *you* don't understand.'' Now, hating herself for showing any vulnerability, she started to cry. "I trusted you. I believed in you, and I thought we had something special. And I *loved* you, you big liar. I loved you so much I thought about the whole big stupid deal, marriage and babies and growing old together and happily ever after. But what I didn't know was that you were and are a total *pig!*''

"Alex—''

"Don't touch me. I'm leaving now. I'm going to do this wedding, get this whole thing over with, then I'm going back to the library and getting my books back and never, *ever* trusting my instincts again.''

"Books? Alex, what are you talking about?''

"This is obviously a foreign conversation to you, because most women were probably totally taken in by the whole act. Well, not this babe! I'm walking out that door and after this wedding is over, I *never, ever* want to see you again!''

She'd done it, pushed him past the brink. His eyes had darkened, his jaw was tightening.

"So you don't want to hear my side of it?''

"I wasn't aware that pigs could talk. Maybe if you oinked a few bars—''

"Get out.''

"With pleasure!''

The door made a resounding slam, but Alex was only halfway down to her floor in the elevator when she burst into tears.

AT FOUR IN THE MORNING, Sean finished the last of a bottle of fine Scotch, then lay back down and stared at the ceiling.

Pig? What the hell was she talking about?

Though it was a totally ungentlemanly thing to do and actually quite sexist, he wondered if Alex was premenstrual.

AT 4:10 IN THE MORNING, Alex finished the last of an incredible piece of chocolate whipped-cream cake, then lay back down and stared at the ceiling.

I realize it was a bit of deception... What the hell was he talking about?

Though it was a totally unladylike thing to do and actually quite sexist, she wondered if Sean's morals were between his legs and if the part of his anatomy in question truly had no conscience.

AND IN NEW HAMPSHIRE, early that same morning, it finally stopped snowing.

Chapter Twelve

"You can go now, Phil. Colonel Brimley flew into Washington this morning and opened the bidding."

"It's too late." Phillip was sitting at the kitchen table, nursing the last of a bottle of good Scotch. He'd blown it. Totally. He wasn't sure exactly what Sean and Muffy were going to do, but he knew one thing for certain.

He'd failed Muffy. Left her alone to face that travesty of a mother. What was Sean supposed to do, marry Muffy? Even friendship didn't extend that far.

He glanced at his watch. Almost noon. The wedding began at three. He'd never make it in three hours.

He gave up.

He was resting his head on the table, his brain in an alcoholic fog, when he felt his shoulder shaking. No, maybe someone was shaking it for him.

"Phil, what the hell are you doing! You can go!"

"Too late," he mumbled.

"I thought you said the wedding began at three."

"It does."

"Well, if you get off your butt and stop feeling sorry for yourself, you can just make it."

He glanced up at her. "I'm not Superman. I can't fly across the continent in three hours. Besides, it's too near Christmas. All the flights are booked up."

"Well, aren't we feeling sorry for ourselves?"

"Go away." For once, he didn't want Rachel's cool competence anywhere near him.

"How about figuring out the time change, which gives you *six* hours to get there, and adding in the company jet and a helicopter ride in from LAX?"

Slowly, ever so carefully, he lifted his head.

"You're kidding."

"Nope. I explained that you were late to your own wedding. The company wants to bend over backward because you were so accommodating while you were forced to stay here."

"Oh my God! Muffy! I've got to pack. Where's my suit?"

"No time. Here's your jacket. Bill, Stan, get him to the jet. And sober him up on the way!"

ALEX, YOU LOOK LIKE—"

"Thanks, Marcy. Got any tricks in that bag of yours that'll make me look halfway decent?"

Today was Saturday, and no one was in the office except Marcy catching up on some of her work. She had reverted to the Marcy of old. In honor of the wedding, she'd dragged out the costume she usually only wore for the Renaissance Faire. She looked like a milkmaid, with her long dress and stomacher. Her hair was in soft ringlets, and there was a circlet of roses on top of her head.

"I'll do anything, Alex. I'll even carry in the pheasants. I just want to get a look at everything."

"Okay."

"Now I know something's wrong. Did you and Sean have a fight?"

"He's history."

"I get it. Well, I'll be up here, and if you see a suitable opening, make sure you buzz me. I just want to see how all of this is done. And Alex?"

"Yeah."

"I'm really sorry. About you and Sean, I mean."

"Ah, I'll be all right."

PHILLIP WAS OVER Texas before he thought about calling Sean.

"Is there a phone on this thing?"

"Sure." Stan and Bill exchanged looks. They hadn't exactly sobered Phillip up. If anything, the guy was so nervous he'd been hitting the bar pretty regularly.

"Would one of you dial Los Angeles information for me?"

THE PHONE RANG, the sound echoing hollowly through the empty Malibu beach house. Ten times, then twelve. Then silence.

"HEY, LOOK UP the hotel. The—the Biltmore, that's it."

Stan and Bill exchanged glances, then dialed Los Angeles information again.

A PIG, EH? Well, I'm going to have my say before this day is over.

Sean was still angry as he stood beneath the stinging, cold spray. The Scotch had definitely been a major mistake. All that was on his mind was getting through this fiasco of a wedding—and he still didn't know exactly what the hell he was going to do if Phillip didn't show—and then cornering little miss know-it-all and letting her know exactly what he thought of her.

The shower was so loud, he didn't hear the ringing phone.

"MAYBE—MAYBE HE'S NOT staying in the Presidential Suite."

"Hey, Phil, buddy, slow down on those Scotch and sodas. Are you sure there's a wedding going on at all, or was it just some ruse to ditch that lousy weather and head out for the coast?"

"No. No, I'm not making this up. Please, I've got to get ahold of Sean."

Stan looked at Bill. Bill scratched his head and looked back at Stan.

"Maybe the hotel directory."

They dialed again and reached the front desk. Bill put his hand over the receiver.

"How about the catering office, Phil? Maybe someone there can reach him?"

Phillip nodded, then turned quite pale as he realized he was going to be sick.

"CATERING OFFICES, the Biltmore. Can I help you?" Marcy didn't mind slipping into her old role on a Saturday.

"Who is this? What? Wait, talk slower, this is kind of—*What!* Phil, Phil, slow down, I can't understand what it is you're saying."

Within minutes, Marcy knew the entire story.

"Yes. Yes, I'll get the message to Sean. That's right, you can land the helicopter on the hotel helipad. I'll be up there waiting for you as soon as I get the message to Sean. Calm down, calm down..."

"SHE'S HYSTERICAL, Ms. Michaels, you've got to help her."

"Don't tell her mother. I'll take care of it."

The bridesmaid looked really concerned, and Alex swiftly followed her to the small room where Muffy was getting ready.

The sight that met her eyes was heartbreaking. Muffy, still in her slip, was sitting on a small stool and sobbing.

"Muffy," Alex said softly, "Muffy, you're going to make yourself sick." Then, glancing quickly around so she was sure no one was within earshot, she said, "Think of the baby."

Muffy grabbed both her hands. Her eyes were rimmed in pink, her ears and nose were the same color, and Alex thought of a small, frightened rabbit she had seen at the London Zoo.

"I can't do this. I can't go out there in front of all those people. I don't know what I'm going to do. Nothing is happening the way I thought it would."

"Muffy, you've got to get a hold of yourself—"

"No, you don't understand. I can't marry Sean. There's someone else."

And Alex, holding Muffy's hands and looking at this gentle little creature, suddenly knew exactly how Scarlett had felt at Melanie's deathbed.

"Muffy, no. Believe me, there isn't."

"There is! Oh, I know Sean has been strong for me and tried to make everything all right, but I don't know what he's going to do now! He didn't count on anything happening this way."

"He's a big boy. He's got to face up to his responsibilities."

Muffy started to sob again as two of her bridesmaids crowded closer, murmuring words of comfort.

"I can't marry Sean, I can't. I can't because I don't love him, I—"

A total, absolute silence descended in the dressing room, and Alex knew, without looking up, that Constance Bradford had come in the door.

"Get out. Everyone get out." Her tone was clipped, her voice that of a woman who was used to being obeyed.

The bridesmaids scattered, their slippered feet pattering over the carpet like a hastily thrown-together rendition of *Swan Lake*.

"That means you, too, Alex."

Alex stood, Muffy still clinging to her hand like an anxious toddler.

"No."

"Get out right this minute or I'll have you fired faster—"

The door opened then, and John Bradford poked his balding head in.

"Muffy? Is everything all right?"

The girl tried to muffle a sob, but John heard the sound and entered the room.

"Muffy, what's wrong?"

"I can't, Daddy. I just c-can't."

"It's all right, darling. You don't have to do anything you don't want to do."

"Oh, John, it's just a simple case of bridal nerves. She'll be ready in about ten minutes. Every woman goes through this, isn't that right, Alex?"

Alex swallowed. She couldn't answer. This woman was thousands of times more horrible than even she had imagined.

"You just remember, Muffy, I'll love you no matter what you decide to do. I want my little girl to be happy, all right?"

"Okay, Daddy."

And Alex felt her throat tightening even more at the look of absolute love on John Bradford's face.

Once he left, it was a different story altogether.

"Get up." Constance grabbed Muffy's elbow and yanked her to her feet, causing her to let go of Alex's hand. "If you think you're going to ruin everything with that pathetic little performance, young lady, just be sure you're willing to pay the price. I will make your life a living hell if you don't marry Sean Lawton!"

And Alex saw it all, the terror in Muffy's eyes, the barely restrained violence in Constance's.

"I can't, I don't love him, I love—"

The hand came up before Alex could do anything about it, and Constance's palm cracked across Muffy's fragile cheekbone. She fell awkwardly, and Alex was down beside her in an instant.

"Get her dressed. Right now. I'm standing here until she walks out that door."

And Alex, knowing she was trapped with one sick cookie, reached for the lace confection that was Muffy's bridal gown.

"BOY, I'LL BET that's pretty difficult, holding those pheasants that way." Marcy's voice was full of admiration.

The boy's chest puffed up with pride. He couldn't have been a day over seventeen. "Yeah, it is."

"Would you show me?"

He glanced around, clearly nervous. "I don't think I'd better."

Marcy smiled, the note she had for Sean Lawton feeling like it was burning a hole in her pocket. She couldn't get inside without a formal invitation. Security was tight since Constance thought the press was rather tacky and she wanted to be able to control which photographs reached the public.

"A big, strong guy like you, afraid to show me how to hold your pheasant?" Her eyelashes fluttered suggestively.

His eyes started to glaze over, and she knew she had him. She'd never met a man who could resist a little feminine persuasion.

"Okay, you put your left hand here, like this..."

She looked up at him, then moved a little closer, just for good measure, and wondered if what she was about to do would merit a raise.

THE VEIL COVERED Muffy's face so no one could see the redness of her eyes.

The three seamstresses had been called in, and those final stitches had ensured a perfect fit.

Now, all that was on Alex's mind was getting Muffy out of striking range of her mother.

"Well, Alex, we have a wedding to run, don't we?" Constance's blue eyes were cold. It was no-holds-barred now that Alex had seen her slap Muffy.

"I'm not leaving her alone with you." Alex could feel Muffy trembling behind her.

"That's fine with me. Muffy's not going to do anything foolish now, are you, dear?"

"No." The one word was barely a whisper.

"He can give you everything, Muffy. The houses, the cars, the clothes, fabulous trips on the yacht. Everything you'd ever want."

Except love, Alex thought, and she was surprised to find her eyes welling with tears.

"Your father will be here in just a few seconds to walk you down the aisle. No matter what he says, we aren't going to say no, are we?"

This was so sick, Alex had to look down at the floor, away from Constance.

"No."

"You'll thank me for this, darling. I know Sean is a very...masculine man, but there are ways of bringing him to heel. I'll teach you."

And with that, Constance turned and walked out of the room.

"Thanks, Alex."

"Muffy, I feel so awful, I never would have planned any of this if I'd known you didn't—"

"Muffy? Are you coming?"

"It's okay, Alex." The pink-rimmed eyes were tired and resigned.

And at that moment, Alex knew Muffy had given up.

"WHAT TIME IS IT, Charlie?"

"Three-fifteen."

"The wedding's running late."

Colleen glanced around unobtrusively, trying to catch a glimpse of her niece. But Alex was nowhere to be found.

"I hope this all works out," she said softly.

"It will, darling, it will."

The crowd began to murmur as Sean and his brother, Brian, came in a side door and approached the altar.

Colleen squeezed Charlie's hand, closed her eyes and uttered a silent prayer.

"HEY, STAN, we're landing in ten minutes. I think we'd better get him sobered up."

"Coffee?"

"Nope. Make him a sandwich while I dump this cold water over his head."

THE TRUMPETS BEGUN to play right on cue, just as Marcy had known they would.

"Hey!" The seventeen-year-old began to panic. "Give me back that bird!"

"Oh, no—"

And Marcy was swept into the procession entering the Crystal Room, just as she had known she would be.

And she knew the procession went right by Sean Lawton.

She patted the note with her free hand and kept time with the stately music as she passed the back row of chairs full of excited guests.

IT HAD BEGAN. The wedding of the year.

And Alex felt absolutely nothing.

Funny how life worked. When something was taken away from you, something was always given back in its place. She might have lost Sean, but after that scene in Muffy's dressing room, she'd forgiven her own mother completely.

Constance Bradford was a monster. Meredith Michaels had done what she thought was best.

There was no comparison.

The trumpets had sounded, the procession was under way. Everything was going perfectly, and two people who didn't love each other were going to be joined together forever in holy matrimony.

Don't think about it.

She refused to look up at the altar, refused to see Sean. She knew Colleen had to be looking for her, but this was an impossible situation.

Leave. You've done enough.

It was then, in the midst of the group of young men leading the Renaissance procession, that she saw Marcy.

SEAN SAW HER at almost the same time, and his first reaction was surprise. Was Marcy supposed to be in the parade? She was carrying a pheasant with a firm grip and trying to catch his attention with her eyes.

Their eyes met. She glanced down.

He saw the small scrap of paper in her hand. The relief he felt was so overwhelming he thought for a minute he was going to pass out.

And as Marcy passed Sean, in the midst of this Renaissance marching band, she slipped him the note, then smiled to a shocked Constance in the front row and skipped merrily on her way.

Sean knew Constance hadn't seen the exchange. He glanced down at the note in his palm, worked it open slowly with his thumb, and read it.

Hang in there, Father Lawton. The cavalry is coming!

And he smiled.

ALEX CHOSE that exact moment to glance at Sean.

He's smiling. How dare he?

She was as close to berserk as she'd ever been in her life, with the exception of last night in Sean's suite. What was Marcy doing in the Renaissance parade? Why was Sean grinning like a real groom? And Muffy...

As if on cue, fife and drum quieted down and the harpist began to play the familiar strains of the "Wedding March."

I can't bear it.

But she couldn't tear herself away. Muffy looked ethereal, a vision in lace, so delicate and fragile.

Sean, the rat, didn't look half bad in his tuxedo.

The crowd was silent. This was what they had come for. This was the event of the Christmas season, and they were going to relish every second of it.

This is the worst day of the rest of my life.

"OKAY, BUDDY, into the helicopter!"

"Oh, God, I don't think I can do this!"

"C'mon, do it for what's her name—Fluffy?"

"Muffy!"

Phillip jumped into the helicopter, fastened his seat belt and closed his eyes.

"DEARLY BELOVED, we are gathered here today..."

Alex rarely cried at weddings, but she could already feel tears gathering in her eyes. She couldn't leave, even to go to find Marcy and ask her why she had chosen such an unorthodox way of taking a look at a large formal wedding.

She couldn't take her eyes off Sean.

They did make a striking couple. She was so delicate and fair; he was so tall and dark. Even from where she stood, Alex could tell that Muffy was leaning on Sean and he was supporting her with his strength.

She couldn't even be jealous of Muffy because she knew the girl was in pain. And what was it she had said?

I don't love Sean. I love—

*What a mess. She doesn't love Sean; he doesn't love her,
I still love him, and who knows if he still loves me or who in
God's name loves Muffy....*

Definitely the wedding of the year.

She'd known it was going to be hard to listen to the ceremony, but she'd had no idea how painful the actual words
were going to be.

"Do you, Elizabeth Anne Bradford, take this man to be
your lawfully wedded husband, for better or worse, in sick-
ness and in health..."

Muffy's quiet "I do" was barely audible in the absolutely quiet Crystal Ballroom.

"Do you, Sean Lawton—"

Alex bit her lip, hard, but the tears started to roll down
her cheeks.

"—to be your lawfully wedded wife—"

Alex swiped unobtrusively at her eyes.

Get it over with.

"—as long as you both shall live?"

"I—"

Alex glanced up, her eyes wide, as she realized Sean was
hesitating.

"I—" Sean suddenly turned around and faced the crowd,
an ashen-faced Muffy leaning heavily against him.

There was a slight rustle in the crowd, and one or two
people couldn't resist whispering.

"I—want you all to know there's been a slight change of
plans. I'm not the groom—he'll be arriving shortly. But in
the meantime, I'd like to tell you about a boy and girl who
grew up together and faced the most unbelievable odds to be
together."

Now, utter pandemonium broke out, excited murmurs
were racing across the crowd. Alex, in total shock, still had
the presence of mind to crane her neck to see the one face
she couldn't wait to get a look at.

Constance Bradford was turning a very nice shade of purple. Lovely.

Sean continued, his voice low and soothing. The crowd began to quiet, not wanting to miss a word of this story.

"She was all of twelve years old when she told me she wanted to spend the rest of her life with this man. He fell in love with her at the same time, with her gentleness, her beauty..."

"COME ON, PHIL, there's no time to lose!"

"What do you mean, I have to wear tights? Marcy, no!"

"It'd take too much time to explain. Just put them on."

"...AND SO I AGREED to the deception, knowing that these two wanted to build a life together, knowing they shared the kind of love that comes along only once in a lifetime..."

Alex's mouth was hanging open in shock. This was wilder than anything she'd imagined. But now that he wasn't going to marry Muffy, what was going to happen between her and Sean?

"NOT THE HAT, Marcy!"

"Shut up, Phil, and put it on. I think it adds a certain je ne sais quoi, don't you think?"

"BUT WHAT I didn't count on was falling in love, myself."

Alex couldn't meet his eyes. Her vision was blurring, her eyes were full of tears. Her legs were trembling so she could barely stand, and there was a knot in her stomach the size of a medicine ball.

How could she have ever doubted this man? Here he was, telling hundreds of people that he loved her.

"It was the most painful thing I have ever experienced, having to hurt the woman I love...."

The woman I love.

Alex knew she was a goner.

"C'MON, PHIL, sober up."

"I can't do this."

"Sure you can. Just grab its little foot like this, and follow me."

"SO, TO WIND THIS all up, Phillip should be here any minute, and when he does arrive—"

"No!"

Constance Bradford finally broke, and it was a glorious sight, indeed. Furious, she rushed to the altar and grabbed Sean's other arm.

"Stop it! Stop it! You're going to marry my daughter! She doesn't love that spineless—"

"Yes, I do."

Alex could have wept at the rapturous look on Muffy's plain little face. She'd slowly straightened up and taken her hands away from her face as Sean had begun his little fireside chat, and now she was looking up at him with total adoration.

"You can't do this to me!" Constance screamed. At that exact moment, a member of the press who had sneaked in dressed as a minstrel quickly snapped several shots.

And Alex didn't even try to confiscate the camera.

When the crowd roared, Alex brought her attention back from the photographer to the front of the ballroom, where Sean was stuffing a handkerchief tightly in Constance's mouth. Then, before she had a chance to react, he marched her back to her husband's side.

"John," he said, looking down at the smiling man, "please restrain her."

"I've been trying to for years."

That got the biggest laugh of all.

Sean walked back up to the front of the crowd. Very gently, he lifted Muffy's veil and arranged it back over her head.

"Muffy," he said softly, right before he kissed her, "here's to your future."

The crowd went wild, and Constance, screaming furiously behind the handkerchief wedged firmly in her mouth, couldn't even be heard.

IT WAS THE strangest wedding Alex had ever attended. While she stood in the back of the ballroom watching total pandemonium reign, the servers, at Sean's request, began bringing the guests small plates of canapés and glasses of punch. The crowd was almost back under control until Muffy, looking exactly like Melanie in *Gone With the Wind* when she recognized Ashley walking up the long, dusty road to Tara, screamed, "Phillip!"

As she picked up the long bridal skirt and train with one hand and began to run toward a tall, lanky blonde dressed in complete Renaissance garb, her face lit up with the purest of emotions, a love so complete and overwhelming it almost hurt to look at her face.

Muffy was beautiful.

The crowd broke into spontaneous applause as she fell into his arms and burst into tears.

And Alex, glancing back at Sean, met his eyes and smiled through her tears.

THE REAL WEDDING was just about to get under way when someone from the audience yelled, "Hey, Sean, is she here?"

Alex, knowing exactly who this bozo was talking about, glanced at the nearest door. Even though two tall Renaissance men stood guard by the doorway, she was sure they'd let her out.

Her feet started to move before she gave the matter coherent thought, but Sean was faster. Knowing she looked like a fool and not even caring, Alex broke into a dead run.

When he swept her up into his arms, she seriously thought about killing him. Looking pleased in that way that only a man can, he began to carry her toward the front of the crowd.

"Put me down," she whispered furiously.

"I'm not letting you go again."

"Down. Now. I mean it, Sean. I'll punch you."

"I love you."

She made her hand into a fist, and he whispered, "I'll drop you right on your caboose."

This man, who not six seconds ago she'd been weepily smiling at, now infuriated her to the point of uncurling her fist and smacking him in his smugly grinning face.

But he caught her hand before it reached its target.

"Darling Alex," he whispered, laughter in his voice, "leave me some energy for our honeymoon."

"WHAT ARE YOU crying about?" Charlie asked, putting his arm around Colleen's waist.

She dabbed at her eyes with a lacy handkerchief. "I just love a happy ending. Look at the way they're fighting!"

"I know. Brings back memories, doesn't it?"

"I'm just glad," said Colleen, "that they're off to such a good start."

SEAN SET Alex down in front of eight hundred people, and she had no choice but to behave herself.

"Are you going to make it a double wedding?" the same bozo called out of the crowd.

"I haven't even asked her," Sean called back. Alex could see that Sean was feeling cocky and on top of the world.

"Why don't you ask her?" the man called out.

Then all she could see was Sean's blue-gray eyes, and suddenly the cockiness was replaced by the slightest vulnerability.

"I was going to ask you, Alex. That night I invited you to dinner. Phillip was supposed to have been here by then, and I would have been able to tell you everything. But I couldn't tell you without asking Phillip first."

She stood perfectly still, knowing this was another moment she would remember for the rest of her life.

He fumbled—Sean fumbled!—in his pocket and brought out a small velvet box. Behind her she could hear the crowd straining to hear.

"Whatever it takes, Alex. Down on my knees, whatever you want. Forgive me for what I did, but I couldn't bear the thought of you with another man. I love you, and I want you in my life. Will you marry me, Alexandra?"

And she knew then that she would, if only to hear her name every day, just the way he said it.

But not just yet.

"Down on your knees, huh?"

He began to look worried, then, resigned, he started to kneel.

"No, Sean. Don't." That he had even considered humbling himself in front of this crowd told her everything she needed to know. That she had even contemplated making him do it made her feel like a worm.

"Marry me?"

Now there was nothing but the thought of waking up to that face every morning, seeing those eyes look at her, forever and ever and ever....

When it was this right, it was so easy.

But she couldn't resist.

"Wellll..."

"Alex."

How she loved to torment this man.

"Yes."

There was another burst of applause when he slipped the diamond ring on her finger. They both turned around just in time to see Phillip's incredulous face, hear "A baby?"

come out of his mouth in a strangled voice and watch as he crumpled to the floor of the Crystal Ballroom in a dead faint.

"A FABULOUS WEDDING, dear. My Christie is getting married next June, and I'm going to make an appointment with you on Monday!"

"I don't know when I've had a better time at a wedding, Alex. You really outdid yourself with this one."

Alex smiled as she felt a familiar arm curl around her waist.

"You've been praised enough. Dance with me."

"Whatever you say, Sean." But she put her arms around his neck and leaned against him as Renaissance music wafted around the ballroom.

"Marcy and Brian certainly seem to have hit it off," she said, looking up at him.

"He likes her, Renaissance dress and all." Sean tightened his grip on her ever so slightly, then said softly, "I thought we could catch an evening flight to Vegas, get married and join Phil and Muffy on the yacht when they leave on their honeymoon. How does the Caribbean sound to you?"

"What?" She couldn't resist teasing him. "No formal wedding?"

He rolled his eyes in disgust, and she burst out laughing and buried her face against his chest.

"Alex, we could catch the seven-thirty flight and be married by midnight."

"Boy, you sure are in a hurry. What about my courtship? My engagement party?"

"Alex." The look in his eyes was deadly serious. "I have waited longer for you than I've waited for any other woman in my entire life."

"I should hope so."

"I don't want to wait any longer."

"I'm not asking you to wait."

He looked supremely frustrated that she wasn't following his line of reasoning. "I don't want anything to go wrong. I don't think I could endure it if anything else came between us."

She leaned her cheek against his chest. "Whatever you say."

THEY MADE IT TO Las Vegas, then flew to join Phillip and Muffy on the yacht, which Sean promptly rechristened *Alexandra the Great*.

Harlequin Romance ®

Delightful

Affectionate

Romantic

Emotional

Tender

Original

Daring

Riveting

Enchanting

Adventurous

Moving

Harlequin Romance—the
series that has it all!

HROM-G

HARLEQUIN PRESENTS®

HARLEQUIN PRESENTS
men you won't be able to resist falling in love with...

HARLEQUIN PRESENTS
women who have feelings just like your own...

HARLEQUIN PRESENTS
powerful passion in exotic international settings...

HARLEQUIN PRESENTS
intense, dramatic stories that will keep you turning
to the very last page...

HARLEQUIN PRESENTS
The world's bestselling romance series!

Harlequin® Historical

If you're a serious fan of historical romance,
then you're in luck!

Harlequin Historicals brings you
stories by bestselling authors, rising new stars
and talented first-timers.

Ruth Langan & Theresa Michaels
Mary McBride & Cheryl St. John
Margaret Moore & Merline Lovelace
Julie Tetel & Nina Beaumont
Susan Amarillas & Ana Seymour
Deborah Simmons & Linda Castle
Cassandra Austin & Emily French
Miranda Jarrett & Suzanne Barclay
DeLoras Scott & Laurie Grant...

You'll never run out of favorites.

Harlequin Historicals...they're too good to miss!

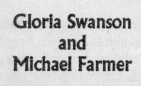

Gloria Swanson
and
Michael Farmer

The renowned actress Gloria Swanson was married a total of six times. She left high school after only one year, moved to Hollywood and married her director, Wallace Beery, in 1916. The marriage lasted about a month. In 1919 she married Herbert K. Somborn, a movie producer and owner of the Brown Derby restaurant. In 1924 she went to France and married Henri, Marquis de la Falaise. The marriage ended after she formed her own production company, and she then married her fourth husband, Michael Farmer, who was known as the Irish Sportsman. Her next marriage, to William N. Davey, an investment broker, again lasted only about forty-five days.

In 1976 Gloria Swanson was married for the last time to William Dufty. He was seventeen years her junior. She died on April 4, 1983, at the age of eighty-four.

B-SWANSON